T H E A T R E   S
A PUBLICATION OF THE SOUTHE

Crosscurrents in the Drama

East and West

Volume 6

Published by the

Southeastern Theatre Conference and

The University of Alabama Press

THEATRE SYMPOSIUM is published annually by the Southeastern Theatre Conference, Inc. (SETC), and by The University of Alabama Press. SETC nonstudent members receive the journal as a part of their membership under rules determined by SETC. For information on membership, write to SETC, P.O. Box 9868, Greensboro, NC 27429-0868. All other inquiries regarding subscriptions, circulation, purchase of individual copies, and requests to reprint materials should be addressed to The University of Alabama Press, Box 870380, Tuscaloosa, AL 35487-0380.

THEATRE SYMPOSIUM publishes works of scholarship resulting from a single-topic meeting held on a southeastern university campus each spring. A call for papers to be presented at that meeting is widely publicized each autumn for the following spring. Authors are therefore not encouraged to send unsolicited manuscripts directly to the editor. Information about the next symposium is available from the new editor, John Frick, Department of Drama, University of Virginia, Charlottesville, Virginia 22903.

THEATRE SYMPOSIUM
A PUBLICATION OF THE SOUTHEASTERN THEATRE CONFERENCE

Volume 6　　　　　　　*Contents*　　　　　　　*1998*

4 CONTENTS

Introduction

IN APRIL 1997, on the campus of the University of Georgia in Athens, a very exciting conference on the "Crosscurrents in the Drama, East and West" took place. The conference brought together some of the finest scholars and artists who concern themselves with the theme of encounters between the very different theatrical cultures of East and West. These cultures had been for so long so completely separated from one another that their mutual discovery, beginning a little over a hundred years ago, has had fascinating and invigorating results, especially in the drama. Theatre has a wonderful capacity to constantly rediscover itself. That rediscovery can have rich consequences when one culture and its theatre meets another culture and its theatre. Misunderstandings can create highly original new forms and styles. Issues arise out of so-called "cultural imperialism." Is there such a thing as appropriating culture in the sense that imperialism appropriates the resources of colonies? This process of mutual discovery also yields parallels in theatre practices and conventions between East and West over history. These are among the subjects explored in the essays here.

I must express my profound thanks to several people. First of all I am grateful to the Office of the Vice President of Academic Affairs, Dr. William Prokasy, at the University of Georgia, for the financial support making it possible to bring six distinguished scholars to campus. These experts—James Brandon, Samuel Leiter, Leonard Pronko, Carol Fisher Sorgenfrei, Andrew Tsubaki, and Farley Richmond—participated in a fascinating panel discussion of the conference's theme. Unfortunately, for reasons of space that discussion could not appear in this volume. I thank Farley Richmond for his assistance in naming other leading scholars who might be invited. The editorial board gave me invaluable advice on the selection and editing of papers. I single out Dr. Samuel Leiter, whose expertise in the field has been inestimable. Selection of papers was a pleasant problem, for there were so many outstanding pieces of scholarship submitted. I must thank my associate editor, Dr. Philip Hill, and my assistant editor, Mick Sokol. I am thankful to the people of The University of Alabama Press for all of their help and in particular to Suzette Griffith and Joe Abbott. And of course, I owe a profound debt to the excellent contributions of the participants in the conference. Many fine papers have had to be excluded from this volume for space considerations, but what is left is an outstanding collection of essays on this subject, and I am proud to have had a part in it.

STANLEY VINCENT LONGMAN
Editor

Some Considerations

of Shakespeare in *Kabuki*

James R. Brandon

*D*URING MOST OF *kabuki*'s history, performance can be characterized by a balance of "*yin* and *yang*." We find fluctuating change and stability, the unknown and the known, the new and the old existing side by side in a balance of unstable *yin* and stable *yang*. For example, in the Tokugawa period (1603–1868), each autumn before the annual *kabuki* season began, the main members of the troupe gathered to select the *sekai,* or worlds, for each of the year's five or six productions. These dramatic worlds were taken from well-known events in history or legend, that is from a stable, received body of knowledge. House playwrights then crafted new plays based on these worlds by fabricating unusual or unexpected plots (*shukô*). In principle every play was "new," with its own unique title, and yet the basic dramatic material was already familiar to audiences. Stable worlds and always-new plots provided a *yin-yang* balance in play creation. I believe that much in *kabuki* can be viewed this way.

Most Japanese and Western observers privilege the traditional, the stable, the positive, the *yang* side of *kabuki*, emphasizing family acting traditions and established conventions of performance. In this brief paper I will focus on the unstable, the uncertain, the indeterminant, the new, the *yin* of *kabuki*, taking as a point of departure the case of *ka-*

This essay elaborates on ideas that were first presented in a paper at the annual convention of the Asian Studies Association of Australia, La Trobe University, 11 July 1996. I am grateful to Ian Carruthers for encouraging me to begin investigating this topic.

buki's engagement with the plays of Shakespeare. The received wisdom is that *kabuki* and Shakespeare have much in common. Indeed, the idea that Shakespeare and *kabuki* naturally go together is something of a cliché.[1] As Kawatake Toshio has pointed out, the two share a similar "baroque" spirit and therefore would seem to be natural partners (1967, 201–2). I suggest here that *kabuki* artists responded to Shakespeare in three radically different ways, none of which satisfactorily fused the unique strengths of Shakespeare (the new, destabilizing, outside *yin* element) with their own theatrical art (the familiar, stable, inside *yang* element). Some of the reasons for these responses we may find in the state of *kabuki* at the time Shakespeare was first introduced to Japan.

Throughout the Tokugawa period, *kabuki* was a popular theatre that purveyed to an eager public dramatic versions of sensational events— recent lovers' suicides, public vendettas, and scandalous murders—much as docudramas on television or gossip items in supermarket tabloids do today. A playwright turned out five or six new plays each year. Actors competed intensely with each other and looked to each play as an opportunity to reach the audience anew. Government decrees ordered theatres to operate in specific theatre districts, so troupes had to vie for the same pool of spectators. In this cutthroat environment actors, playwrights, and producers happily seized on extraordinary contemporary happenings to give them an edge over rivals across the street or down the block.[2]

Let me briefly enumerate some factors that I believe contributed to instability and change in *kabuki*, the *yin* side of the equation.[3] First, on an average, one of the three or four licensed theatres in the city of Edo (Tokyo) burned to ashes every two years. Fire destroyed one or another of the licensed theatres on more than a hundred occasions between 1657 and 1864 (Nojima 1988, Appendix, 27–29). On at least fifteen occasions, one of Edo's theatre licensees was unable to produce, and his

---

[1]Very recent examples are in Pronko (1994, 113–15), Nouryeh (1993, 254–55), and Kennedy (1993, 286–87).

[2]Of course, favorite plays were commonly revived, and each licensed theatre had in its permanent repertory several "house plays" (*waki kyôgen*) performed early in the morning (Brandon 1975, 24) and "memorial plays" (*kinen geki*) performed on ceremonial occasions (Leiter 1979, 204–5).

[3]In the interest of brevity I do not provide specific evidence for each point, but this evidence is available in chronologies and compilations of source material, such as Ihara Toshirô, ed., *Kabuki Nempyô* (Kabuki Chronology), 8 vols. (Tokyo: Iwanami Shoten, 1956–1963) and Kabuki Hyôbanki Kenkyûkai, ed., *Kabuki Hyôbanki Shûsei* (Compilation of Kabuki Actor Critiques), 10 vols. (Tokyo: Iwanami Shoten, 1972–1977).

license devolved to a substitute, who was granted a "reserve license" (*hikae yagura*). These changeovers caused financial distress and considerable instability in the system.

Second, in the formative period of male *kabuki*, through the Genroku period beginning in 1688 and at least into the Hôreki period ending in 1764, acting was a precarious occupation. It may be that as many as three thousand actors competed at any one time in the dozen or so major licensed theatres in Japan's three metropolises (Edo, Osaka, and Kyoto) and in the hundred or so smaller unlicensed theatres that existed in cities and towns throughout the country. Actors were clearly in intense rivalry.

Third, we have ample evidence that major actors and stars moved from one licensed theatre to another and from one major city to another throughout their careers. To illustrate: minor actor Tamagawa Gensaburô moved fourteen times in twenty-eight years, and over a twenty-four-year period Sodesaki Karyû played thirteen different theatres, which entailed moving to another city ten times (Kabuki 1972–1977, Appendix vol., 209, 218). The constant movement of actors among troupes and theatres does not suggest that *kabuki* at that time was a fixed or stable entity.

Fourth, out of nearly 600 acting family names (*myôji*)[4] that we find in the eighteenth century, 575 had disappeared from the *kabuki* world by the twentieth century (Kabuki 1972–1977, Appendix vol., 158–278). What caused this dinosaur-like extinction? A ceaseless rivalry with other actors and a desire to gain an advantage over one's peers, as well as changes in Japanese society, provided strong incentives to experiment with the new. Of course, some actors from traditional families were intensely conservative, but others dared to seek out imaginative, original approaches to *kabuki*.

Therefore, during the Meiji period (1868–1912), when Shakespeare was first brought into Japan as part of the flood of Western culture, *kabuki* had had two and a half centuries of experience in adapting to new circumstances. It wasn't strange for actors and managers to keep *kabuki* up-to-date; they had always done so. In the first two decades of the Meiji era—the 1870s and 1880s—new types of *kabuki* plays were

---

[4]During the Tokugawa period actors and other commoners were forbidden by law to have family names (*myôji*), and government documents always referred to actors by their given names only. But within the theatrical world actors have used both family and given names from the beginning of *kabuki* (Ichikawa Danjûrô, Matsumoto Kôshirô). See, for example, Hattori (1986, 249–52).

created that responded to the influx of European customs, technology, and ideas. At the Shintomi Theatre in 1878, Ichikawa Danjûrô IX (1839–1903), known as the greatest *kabuki* actor of his generation, declared publicly his disgust with traditional *kabuki* plays and acting styles and vowed to "reform"—that is, to Westernize—his art (Ihara 1956–1963, vol. 7, 233–36). He eschewed *kabuki*'s traditional *mie* poses and musical elocution (*yakuharai*). His intellectual advisor, Fukuchi Ôchi, made four overseas missions on behalf of the Meiji government. He saw that Europe's elite patronized ballet and opera, and he wanted *kabuki* to be similarly favored in Japan's modernized culture. He urged dropping old conventions, such as the *hanamichi* and much more.

Danjûrô's contemporary and rival, Onoe Kikugorô V (1844–1903), enthusiastically supported the writing of new plays set in the Meiji present. These were called cropped-hair plays (*zangiri mono*) in reference to the Meiji edict that men must cut off their topknot to be part of the contemporary world. A typical play, Kawatake Shigetoshi notes, would feature cloth umbrellas, shoes, suits and dresses, chapeaux, briefcases, pocket watches, glass carafes, lamps, pistols, and the like (Kawatake 1959, 789–91). Something of the adventurous, offbeat spirit of the cropped-hair plays can be seen in the following example. In 1891 an Englishman named Spencer was making spectacular balloon ascents in Ueno Park in Tokyo. Within months the cropped-hair play *Fûsen Nori Uwasa Takadono* (Riding the Famous Hot-Air Balloon) was written by Kawatake Mokuami and staged at the Kabuki Theatre in Tokyo, starring Kikugorô as Spencer. Suspended from a balloon high in the theatre's rigging, Kikugorô made a speech in English: "Ladies and gentlemen, I have been up three thousand feet. Looking down, I was pleased to see you in this Kabuki Theatre. Thanks [*sic*] you, Ladies and gentlemen, with all my heart, I thank you" (Ihara 1956–1963, vol. 7, 375). When playwrights of the Meiji period created cropped-hair plays and actors changed traditional conventions, they were continuing the usual process in *kabuki* of molding play forms and acting techniques to suit contemporary audiences. *Kabuki* seemed to have moved far in the direction of modernization (and Westernization) in these first fifteen years of the Meiji period. But these cases proved to be exceptions; other actors did not follow Danjûrô's or Kikugorô's examples. By all accounts audiences simply found Danjûrô's new acting style dull. By the end of the 1880s even Kikugorô had abandoned his experiments and no longer did cropped-hair plays.

Nevertheless, *kabuki* playwrights were turning to European drama for ideas, situations, and characters and even for scenes and whole plays that they thought could be adapted to the *kabuki* stage. Some plays used Western locales for the sake of exotic appeal. Other plays adapted stories from Western drama and literature to *kabuki* performance and Japanese settings.

Against this background let us see how *kabuki* initially encountered the plays of Shakespeare. Although certain dramatic sequences suggestive of Shakespeare appear in a handful of Tokugawa-period *kabuki* plays (such as *Merchant of Venice* in 1695 and *Romeo and Juliet* in 1771 and again in 1810), Toyoda Minoru suggests that similarities are the result of coincidence or of the influence of Chinese literary models (1940, 4). Japanese scholars think it is extremely improbable that playwrights before 1868 knew of Shakespeare's plays.

The first *kabuki* production of Shakespeare by professionals in Japan of which we have certain knowledge was an adaptation by Katsu Genzô of *The Merchant of Venice* performed as a domestic play (*sewamono*) at the Ebisu Theatre in Osaka in 1885. Given the fanciful title *Sakura Doki Zeni no Yo no Naka* (A Time of Cherry Blossoms, A World of Money), it was a tremendous success. The production was in the eighteenth year of Meiji, so one could hardly say that Shakespeare had been rushed to the stage. It set the style for a dozen succeeding productions—they were wholly localized, with Japanese characters, and set in Japan. In fact, adapting Shakespeare to the stage in Japan could not have been done earlier. A production at that time relied upon several steps of adaptation, in Japanese and in English, in media other than the stage. This *kabuki* adaptation was four removes from Shakespeare: the production used Genzô's Japanese-language dramatization, which he based on a serial novel by Udagawa Bunkai previously published in the Japanese-language newspaper *Asahi* (Osaka), which in turn was based on an earlier Japanese-language translation of the eighteen-page English-language story from Charles and Mary Lamb's *Tales from Shakespeare* (1807), which, in turn, was based on Shakespeare's play (Kawatake 1974, 498; Ihara 1956–1963, vol. 7, 304; Kawatake 1959, 833; Minami 1996, 1–2; Lamb and Lamb 1892, 104–21).[5] Genzô's adaptation proved enormously successful with at least twelve separate productions in Osaka and Tokyo between 1885 and 1908 (Minami 1996, 2–6; Ihara 1956–1963, vol. 7, 441, 531).

The next two *kabuki* productions of Shakespeare, in 1907 and 1908, were both of Yamagishi Kayô's adaptation of *Hamlet* set in Japan. First, the young actor Ichikawa Kodanji V starred as Hamlet, and the follow-

---

[5] I want to thank Minami Ryûta for allowing me to consult his excellent "A Chronological Table of Shakespearean Productions in Japan," prior to its publication. It has been extremely useful.

ing year, the rising star of *kabuki* in Osaka, Nakamura Ganjirô I (1860–1935), revived the script to considerable success. The adaptation was titled *Hamu Retto*. The hero's pseudo-Japanese name vaguely suggested the exotic; otherwise, the story was wholly localized. The action was placed in Ashikaga-period Japan (fourteenth to sixteenth centuries), and the script was written in traditional, old-fashioned *kabuki* style, with sections of chanted narrative (Kawatake 1974, 216–26). Shakespeare's melancholy Dane was not used to promote a new style of drama or performance in *kabuki*. Photographs of *Hamu Retto* show all the physical attributes of a standard *kabuki* history play—settings, costumes, wigs, makeup, and stage positioning (see Kawatake 1967, before 1).

In these productions, Shakespeare's stories were adapted to fit Japanese culture and *kabuki* theatrical form. Shakespeare's foreign dramatic material was assimilated into *kabuki* dramatic worlds (*sekai*), and characters were presented through traditional *kabuki* acting and staging techniques. Further, the productions were staged in *kabuki* theatres as part of a regular *kabuki* season, and Shakespeare's presence was completely or largely erased.

The second approach to Shakespeare by *kabuki* was to accept Shakespeare's "otherness" and attempt to "replicate" the Western elements of his drama on the Japanese stage. This approach was inspired by new knowledge of modern European dramaturgy and realistic staging that began to filter into Japan in the second and third decades of the twentieth century. In Japan modern theatre was called *shingeki*, literally "new theatre." Attendant on the development of modern theatre in Japan, the vast corpus of Western drama was translated into Japanese language for *shingeki* performance. Ten of Shakespeare's plays were translated into Japanese between 1905 and 1910 by Tosawa Masayasu and Asano Wasaburô (Toyoda 1940, 45–47). Between 1907 and 1928 Tsubouchi Shôyô (1859–1935), professor of English literature at Waseda University, finished his monumental translations of Shakespeare's complete works (Milward 1963, 190–91). Shôyô's translations were widely read and admired. As the new translations (*honyaku*) became available, the older adaptations (*hon'an*) came to be seen as inferior and *kabuki* actors stopped using them. A translation was validated as "following the original text" (*gensaku dôri*), conferring on it the authority of Old Master Shakespeare himself. Here, let me suggest two aspects of translation that I believe had profound and lasting effects on *kabuki* interpretations of Shakespeare.

First, when actors memorized a scholar's translation, they gave up, apparently largely unnoticed, their extremely important power to act spontaneously. Improvisation during performance contributed life and vitality to Tokugawa-period *kabuki*. This is immediately apparent if we read the text of a play in the standard repertory: these texts comprise stage directions (*togaki*) together with dialogue (*serifu*) and lyrics of offstage songs (*uta*) and of chanted narrative (*jôruri*). The stage directions contain many places where the actor is told to do the sequence as he wishes. It was easy for actors to continue their old habits of improvising as long as they were playing Shakespeare in adaptation because the script was in no way sacrosanct. But a translation *was* Shakespeare and was inviolate.

Second, faithful translations stamped the word "foreign" on every page of Shakespeare's plays. In performance "authentic" settings and costumes cried out England, Italy, Scotland, Denmark, Greece—never Japan. Japanese audiences read productions of translations as irrevocably "other." Characters moved and spoke as if they were Europeans motivated by Judeo-Christian beliefs, not as Japanese motivated by Buddhist-Shinto beliefs. The task of the *kabuki* actor doing Shakespeare in translation, then, was to portray a foreigner convincingly—a Danish Hamlet or a Scottish Lady Macbeth. An Englishman's observation that Kôshirô VII's performance as Othello in 1925 was so excellent that "it was in no way different from seeing the play in London and New York" was taken, quite naturally, to be the supreme compliment (Kawatake 1969, 21).

A small number of *kabuki* actors inspired by modern Western theatre chose to perform Shakespeare in translation in the period 1905 to 1925. They did so because Shakespeare was a part of the "modern," that is Western, world they wished to enter. The *kabuki* actor most enamored of Western theatre was Ichikawa Sadanji II (1880–1940). In 1906 at the age of twenty-seven he set off for Europe to see theatre and attend acting school. His eight-month trip to Europe was the first by a *kabuki* actor. He was also the first *kabuki* actor to act abroad: he performed in Moscow and Saint Petersburg at the head of his own troupe in 1928 (*Grand Kabuki*, 1–11). A year after he returned home he performed Shylock in *The Merchant of Venice*, and in 1909 he cofounded the famous Free Theatre (Jiyû Gekijô) with Osanai Kaoru. His aim was to retrain *kabuki* actors to perform modern drama or, as the slogan went, "turn professionals into amateurs" (Komiya 1956, 292). For fifteen years Sadanji and the Free Theatre focused on contemporary Western drama, but in February and October 1925 the group staged Shakespeare, with Sadanji playing major roles in *Julius Caesar* and *Othello*, using new translations by Osanai Kaoru. All major roles were taken by *kabuki* actors. A photograph of Sadanji as Iago shows him dressed in lace collar, velvet jacket, and tights (Kawatake 1969, 20).

The actor Morita Kanya XIII (1885–1932) was eager to bring *kabuki* into the twentieth century. He organized the Literary Arts Theatre (Bungeiza), which became active in 1915. He gathered around him young, reform-minded *kabuki* actors such as Ichikawa Ennosuke II (the second *kabuki* actor to study theatre in Europe) and Ôtani Tomoemon VI. They joined with actresses trained at the Imperial Theatre School for Actresses to study the new modern drama of the West. Kanya's troupe of *kabuki* actors and modern actresses mounted ten productions of new plays and of translated Western drama through 1925. Kanya acted in *Romeo and Juliet,* the group's second production, in 1918 and played a highly acclaimed Hamlet in the group's fourth production in 1919, both in Shôyô's direct translations (Kawatake 1960–1962, vol. 4, photo facing 475, and vol. 5, 134). Typically, Kanya, a thirteenth-generation *kabuki* actor, acted opposite a newly trained *shingeki* actress. These productions attempted to "replicate" British Shakespeare of the period. We can see from photographs of the productions that they do not just deny Japan, but they deny *kabuki* as well. Kanya appears gaunt and dressed in black tights—he is indistinguishable from a canonical English Hamlet (Kawatake 1960–1962, vol. 4, facing 475). Earlier, in the 1880s and 1890s, *kabuki* actors had tried to subsume their adapted Shakespeare into Japanese patterns of *kabuki* performance; now two decades later, Sadanji and Kanya tried to submerge *kabuki* in the European world of Shakespearean drama and theatre. Simply put, when translations were performed, *Japanese* bodies were put to the service of an *English* Shakespeare.

I argue that neither of these approaches to Shakespeare produced fruitful, long-lasting results. The early "localized" Shakespeare productions done in *kabuki* style were ridiculed as vulgar distortions of the works of a foreign dramatic genius. The later "authentic" productions were so far removed from *kabuki* that most actors were not attracted. Indeed, for a period of thirty-five years, from 1925 until 1960, no *kabuki* actor appeared in a play by Shakespeare. It is understandable that Shakespeare's plays would not be performed in Japan during the Second World War, when England was a national enemy, but the rift continued for a decade and a half after the war was over. It was as if the Bard and *kabuki* had been judged incurably incompatible.

But then, beginning in the 1960s, Shakespeare and *kabuki* were brought together in a third kind of relationship. High-profile theatre organizations invited *kabuki* stars to take leading roles in commercial, large-scale productions. The first such production starred Matsumoto Kôshirô VIII (1910–1982) as Othello at Sankei Hall in Tokyo in 1960. In all, major *kabuki* actors have starred in sixteen productions of Shakespeare's greatest works—*King Lear, Richard III, Romeo and Juliet, Macbeth, Hamlet,* and *Othello*—over the past thirty years. This is a significant achievement. These are "important" productions, widely covered in the press, treated respectfully by critics, and sure to sell out houses. However, they are not "*kabuki.*" The *kabuki* actor is not hired because of his ability "to play *kabuki*" but because he has box-office appeal and a powerful stage presence that may carry a big production. All the other roles are played by actors from modern genres—*shingeki,* musical theatre, film, and television—and directors, designers, and choreographers are from outside *kabuki.* We can examine stills, films, and videotapes, as well as live performances, and we can make our own evaluation of the way postwar *kabuki* actors have performed Shakespeare. Almost all of the *kabuki* acting style has been suppressed, and all of *kabuki*'s artistic techniques have been banished in these commercial productions based on translations.[6] The prime movers in this third meeting between Shakespeare and *kabuki* actors are commercial sponsors and theatre organizations—Sunshine Theatre, Nissei Theatre, Sankei Hall, Globe Theatre, Shiki Theatre Company, Kumo Theatre Company, Tôhô Theatrical Corporation, and Shôchiku Theatrical Corporation. Other than Shôchiku, these groups do not have connections with *kabuki,* nor have they any particular knowledge of it. The great *kabuki* actor Onoe Shôroku II (1913–1989) understood very well his position when he played Othello in 1969. A famously blunt and forthright man, he promised in a published interview, "I will work to avoid playing in a *kabuki* manner" (Onoe and Asari 1969, 6).

The productions do not use *kabuki* techniques of acting, staging, music, costuming, or makeup. What are these performances then? At heart they are realistic *shingeki* productions that happen to have a *kabuki* star in a leading role. That actor brings poise, physical control, and a powerful voice to his acting. But the productions are designed to replicate some English model. These productions have no room for *kabuki* within their representation of Shakespeare's exotic foreignness.

We can note one important exception to this record of missed chances: the brilliant *kabuki* actor of female roles, Bandô Tamasaburô V (b. 1950), whose appearances in Shakespeare in 1976, 1977, and 1978

---

[6]Many of the performances are on videotape. A documentary was telecast in September 1994 about the three generations of Matsumoto Kôshirô who played Othello. The program contains still photos of Kôshirô VII in 1925, film clips of his son Kôshirô VIII in 1960, and the complete stage production of his grandson Kôshirô IX in 1994, none of which show the actors deploying identifiable *kabuki* acting techniques.

were extravagantly, and I think rightly, praised. Surrounded by the usual cast of modern drama actors, he projected an intense presence that was nearly overwhelming. I was fortunate to see Tamasaburô as Lady Macbeth in 1976, and I still retain a clear memory of his majestic, yet delicate, carriage and his steely, insinuating *onnagata* voice. I suppose he was not "playing *kabuki*," but he brought his *kabuki* sense and technique to bear on the role much more directly than other *kabuki* actors have done. He stood out against the bland, lifeless, and powerless *shingeki* performers surrounding him.

In summary, when *kabuki* first encountered the plays of Shakespeare in the 1880s and 1890s, his "new" stories were adapted, readapted, revised, re-revised, and enfolded into well-known Japanese dramatic worlds (*sekai*). The stories were played as traditional *kabuki* theatre in a manner that almost wholly "Japanized" them. Shakespeare's foreignness was deliberately obliterated in the process. Then, in the first two decades of the twentieth century, the most modern-minded *kabuki* actors tried to play Shakespeare in the Western fashion of spoken *shingeki* drama. They were inspired by the *difference* they perceived between modern Western realism and *kabuki*. In this second approach lie several paradoxes, hardly recognized at the time. Surely it is a profound paradox that Shôyô and other Meiji scholars used Shakespeare to speak for Japan's modern present, when in fact the Old Master represented a European past that was several centuries dead by then. Another paradox, and one with dire practical consequences for *kabuki*, was that even though Sadanji, Kanya, and Kôshirô did not use *kabuki* performing techniques, they nonetheless were imbued with the basic *kabuki* attitude that new material could be incorporated into *kabuki*. They were using the social institution of *kabuki* to "try on" Western patterns of life, to stay up-to-date, all within the *kabuki* system. Because *kabuki* actors regularly acted in new material, it was not immediately understood that Shakespeare contained no links to the Japanese past. Could the new material be integrated into *kabuki* if there were no known *sekai* into which Shakespeare's stories could fit? An important link was missing in the chain. And a final paradox was that the *kabuki* actor of the 1920s, a master of highly developed codes of music, dance, and acting (*kata*), was expected to replicate realistically the behavior and customs of Europeans. Could he do this and still function as a *kabuki* actor? It seems to me these were all insurmountable dilemmas. In the end, neither the early efforts to assimilate nor the later efforts to replicate were sustainable. By the 1920s, the production system of *kabuki* could not provide a viable milieu for Shakespeare productions. And it can be said that when *kabuki* gave up on Shakespeare and other Western drama, it also withdrew from modern Japan. After this, contemporary events in Japanese life would be excluded from the *kabuki* stage. Japan's present, including Shakespeare, who was a part of Japan's modernity, would be left to *shimpa*[7] and *shingeki,* then to the movies and television. As Kawatake Shigetoshi has written, by the 1920s "*kabuki* surrendered" modernity to *shingeki* and "changed from its original status as a modern drama to become a traditional theatre" (1959, 1064).

I personally regret that *kabuki* actors do not apply their prodigious performing technique to Shakespeare today. Such attempts wouldn't necessarily meet with success, however. Shakespeare's dramatic world and *kabuki*'s theatrical world are not identical, in spite of Shôyô's statement. But they may be complementary. Their meeting might produce greatness if each added its special strength to the union. *King Lear* has been performed as *kathakali* dance-drama in India and *The Winter's Tale* as Yueju opera in China. One brilliant application of Asian traditional performing techniques to Shakespeare was the production of *Kunqu Macbeth.* Chinese opera actors used all of their techniques of song and declamatory speech, of costuming and stylized makeup, and of conventionalized gesture and acrobatic fighting movements. Audiences in China in 1986 and in Europe in 1987 were thrilled by how Chinese opera had vitalized Shakespeare's drama.

Who am I, an American outside the world of *kabuki,* to carp that *kabuki* actors from the 1960s through the 1990s are not interested in performing Shakespeare in "their" style? Am I imposing my own agenda by raising the question? My point is simple: if *kabuki* actors are going to perform Shakespeare today, isn't their strong suit playing him as *kabuki,* using the art they know? Isn't that more sensible than *kabuki* actors doing Shakespeare as *shingeki,* a style they *don't* know?

Works Cited

Japanese names are referenced in Japanese fashion, family name first without a comma before the given name.
Abé Yûzô. 1970. *Tokyo no Koshibai* (Tokyo's Unlicensed Theatres). Tokyo: Engeki Shuppansha.
Bandô Tamasaburô and Ohkura Shunji. 1983. *Onnagata.* Tokyo: Heibonsha.
Brandon, James R. 1975. *Kabuki: Five Classic Plays.* Cambridge: Harvard University Press (New edition, Honolulu: University of Hawaii Press, 1992).
Grand Kabuki Overseas Tours: 1928–1993. 1994. Tokyo: Shochiku Co.

---

[7]Directors and actors in the intermediate theatre form, *shimpa,* literally "new style," produced many of Shakespeare's plays in the Meiji period.

Hattori Yukio. 1986. *Ôi Naru Koya* (The Prodigious Playhouse). Tokyo: Heibonsha.

——. 1993. *Edo Kabuki* (Kabuki in the City of Edo). Tokyo: Iwanami Shoten.

Ihara Toshirô. 1933. *Meiji Engekishi* (History of Meiji Theatre). Tokyo: Hô Shuppan.

——, ed. 1956–1963. *Kabuki Nempyô* (Kabuki Chronology). 8 vols. Tokyo: Iwanami Shoten.

Kabuki Hyôbanki Kenkyûkai, ed. 1972–1977. *Kabuki Hyôbanki Shûsei* (Compilation of Kabuki Actor Critiques). 10 vols. Tokyo: Iwanami Shoten.

Kawatake Shigetoshi. 1959. *Nihon Engeki Zenshi* (History of Japanese Theatre). Tokyo: Iwanami Shoten.

Kawatake Shigetoshi et al., eds. 1960–1962. *Engeki Hyakka Daijiten* (Encyclopedia of Theatre). 6 vols. Tokyo: Heibonsha.

Kawatake Toshio. 1967. *Hikaku Engekigaku* (Study of Comparative Drama). Tokyo: Nansôsha.

——. 1969. "Nihon no 'Oserô' " (Japan's "Othello"). In *Nissei Gekijô Program,* no. 62 (March), 20–21. Tokyo: Nissei Gekijô.

——. 1974. *Zoku Hikaku Engekigaku* (Study of Comparative Drama Continued). Tokyo: Nansôsha.

Kennedy, Dennis. 1993. *Looking at Shakespeare: A Visual History of Twentieth-Century Performance.* Cambridge: Cambridge University Press.

Komiya Toyotaka, comp. and ed. 1956. *Japanese Music and Drama in the Meiji Era.* Translated by Edward G. Seidensticker and Donald Keene. Tokyo: Ôbunsha.

Lamb, Charles, and Mary Lamb. 1892. *Tales from Shakespeare* (1807). London and New York: Macmillan.

Leiter, Samuel L. 1979. *Kabuki Encyclopedia: An English-Language Adaptation of Kabuki Jiten.* Westport, Conn.: Greenwood Press.

Milward, Peter. 1963. "Shakespeare in Japanese." In *Studies in Japanese Culture: Tradition and Experiment,* ed. Joseph Roggendorf. Tokyo: Sophia University.

Minami Ryûta. 1996. "A Chronological Table of Shakespearean Productions in Japan." Unpub. manuscript.

Nissei Gekijô. 1972. *Nissei Gekijô Program,* no. 6. Tokyo.

Nojima Jûsaburô, ed. 1988. *Kabuki Jinmei Jiten* (Biographical Dictionary of Kabuki). Tokyo: Nichigai Associates.

Nouryeh, Andrea J. 1993. "Shakespeare and the Japanese Stage." In *Foreign Shakespeare: Contemporary Performance,* ed. Dennis Kennedy. Cambridge: Cambridge University Press.

Pronko, Leonard C. 1994. "Creating Kabuki for the West." In *Contemporary Theatre Review* I, part 2:113–15.

Onoe Shôroku, and Asari Keita. 1969. " 'Osero' de no Kokoromi" ("Othello," an Experiment). In *Nissei Gekijô Program,* no. 62 (March), 4–6. Tokyo: Nissei Gekijô.

Toita Yasuji, ed. 1955. *Kabuki Meisakusen* (Selection of Kabuki Masterpieces). Vol. 1. Tokyo: Sôgensha.

Toyoda Minoru. 1940. *Shakespeare in Japan: An Historical Survey.* Tokyo: Published for the Shakespeare Association of Japan by Iwanami Shoten.

From the London Patents

to the Edo *Sanza*

A Partial Comparison of the British Stage
and *Kabuki,* ca. 1650–1800

Samuel L. Leiter

*I*T IS A SOURCE of never-ending wonder to discover that widely disparate cultures often have created remarkably similar artifacts and institutions. In the realm of theatre history we are especially fascinated by comparative studies that examine the resemblances and differences between the West and the East, as, for example, between Aristotle and Bharata, Aeschylus and Zeami, and Shakespeare and Chikamatsu, or between such forms as *nô* and Greek theatre, and *kabuki* and Elizabethan theatre, and so forth. Does not a large part of this fascination stem from the thrill of realizing that there are certain threads that constitute what it is to be human, and that these threads often tie us together with peoples to whom we might not otherwise have felt thus connected? If so, how much more exciting must it be when cultures thought profoundly dissimilar prove, under their external differences, to have remarkable kinship.

A prime example of this phenomenon is the premodern Japanese and English theatre. Most previous comparisons of these national theatres have focused on the work of playwrights Shakespeare and Chikamatsu, or on the staging methods of the *kabuki* and Elizabethan theatres, or on similarities between *nô* and the medieval stage (see Pronko 1967, Fujita and Pronko 1996, and Tsubouchi 1960). Little attention has been

I wish to thank Dr. James R. Brandon for his helpful comments on an earlier draft of this article.

paid, though, to the even more striking correspondences between *ka-buki* and the English theatre from roughly 1650 to 1800. This seems a far more fertile ground for investigation not only because of their chronological coexistence but also because the period offers a compelling picture of two similar and tantalizingly comparable theatrical cultures, coexisting on islands at opposite ends of the world, with only the slightest knowledge of one another.

What were some of these shared features? In both countries, theatrical business was highly commercialized and expensive, controlled to a great extent by manager-actors and their business representatives. They were devoted to annual seasons of nonreligious performances, new and revived, and made use of print media to advertise their wares. Audiences were composed primarily of an urban mercantile class mixed with aristocrats, and many spectators sat on the stage itself. At the beginning of the period, the theatre was allowed to resume performances after having been closed down by the authorities, and it continued to operate under an ever-censorious government's eye. The government strictly limited the number of licensed, competing playhouses, which had to fight for audiences not only with one another but with various unofficial minor theatres. The profession promoted the skills of highly paid stars, many of whom established a company system of actor-management, and the public lionized actors while considering them socially inferior. Actors closely modeled their interpretations on those of their predecessors, and roles were distributed according to specializations. Among some actors' specialties was the ability to play roles of the opposite sex. Performances were held in box, pit, and gallery theatres using a stage employing a front curtain, apron, and technically advanced mechanical devices for scene shifting and special effects. The changeable scenery was sometimes fantastical and sometimes relatively realistic and was composed of platforms and flats that could be instantly transformed before the audience's eyes. Dramas often incorporated musical accompaniment and dancing. A flourishing tradition of strolling players brought theatre to the countryside. Moreover, the period saw theatre criticism experience its birth pangs.

This list—covering the seven broad groupings of management, government regulation, actors, audiences, architecture/stage machinery, repertory, and criticism—provides a sturdy platform from which to compare the English and Japanese theatres of the mid–seventeenth through eighteenth centuries.[1] Of course, several of these character-

---

[1] I know of one previous attempt at a similar comparison: David Waterhouse, "Actors,

istics could be found in a few other Asian countries but certainly not in aggregate and not during the period being discussed here.[2] Because of space limitations, I will look at only three of these areas: government regulation, actors, and the combined area of theatre architecture and scenography (including special effects and lighting).[3] Although I will discuss the world of actors, I will have to eliminate comparative discussion of the potentially rich topic of acting methods. What remains will still reveal not only distinct parallels but, just as important, significant differences that allow us to gain an even clearer picture of the theatres of these widely separated nations during the period in question.

The dates covered are not, of course, precisely symmetrical but are close enough to be of interest. The English side begins with the Restoration (1660–1700), the Japanese with the Jôo era (1652-1655), although the period that most closely parallels the Restoration is Genroku (technically 1688-1703 or 1704 but usually widened to include the period from 1670 to the 1730s).

England and Japan share certain historical and cultural resemblances beyond their approaches to theatre. Their existence as culturally advanced island nations offshore from enormously vital and tremendously influential mainland societies—from which they nevertheless managed to maintain a powerful sense of difference—surely might be plumbed, if only teasingly, for answers to the riddle of why so many similarities

---

Artists and the Stage in Eighteenth-Century England." However, the essay, which Waterhouse admits is "hasty, rambling, and incomplete," is so riddled with problems of substance and fact that I believe a fresh look is warranted. Richard Southern makes some brief but interesting comparisons between scenic developments of the classical Japanese (*nô* and *kabuki*) and English theatres of roughly the same periods (1976, 117–18).

[2] I am grateful to Dr. Kathy Foley for verifying the validity of this statement.

[3] The original version of this essay contained a comparison of managerial methods. Omitted here because of space considerations, it touched on the similarities and differences in the managerial hierarchies that ran the theatres on a day-by-day basis; the relative profitability of London's theatre business contrasted with the frequent bankruptcies of Japanese producers; the use of an alternative management system (*hikae yagura*) for troubled theatres in Japan; the shared dependence on box-office income supplemented by outside investors; resemblances and divergences in the average annual season (for example, London theatres performed 210 nights over eight months; Japanese theatres operated 220 days over eleven months); the position of long runs (more prevalent in Japan than in England, whose long-standing record of a 62-performance run of *The Beggar's Opera* [1728] was overshadowed by such examples as the 280 showings of *Okama Akinai Soga* [1721]); and each country's methods of advertising, as in posters, programs, onstage announcements, billboards. For background on Japanese methods, see entries in Leiter 1997a for Benzuke, 42; Chômoto, 62; Hikae Yagura, 163; Kanban, 275; Kôgyô, 338; Nadai, 427; Zagashira, 719; and Zamoto, 719. For British methods, see Milhous 1980.

arose. Within the fifty-to-seventy-five-year period preceding that covered here, each nation had experienced a shift from an agrarian to a highly commercialized, consumer-oriented urban society, with the consequent growth of a sophisticated townsman culture. On the other hand, England, having defeated the Spaniards, was feeling its expansionist oats, whereas Japan, having established the Tokugawa shôgunate, isolated itself from the world; each position led to remarkable cultural developments. As Yamazaki Masakazu has explained recently (1994), the premodern Japanese were actually more humanistically individualistic than has been previously thought, and they shared many cultural affinities with the West. Searching for answers to the riddle in such events and affinities will always remain pure speculation, giving off heat if not much light. Ultimately, the causes for such parallelism can never be ascertained, and the role of pure coincidence must definitely be allowed in the majority of correspondences cited. Yet the very existence of correspondences is intriguing to ponder if only because it offers a means to understanding what may, at first, seem too much "the other" for ready comprehension. Likewise, and perhaps ironically, seeing the eighteenth-century English theatre held up to its Asian mirror may allow us to view it in a new and illuminating light.

Government Regulations

Managers in both England and Japan had to endure the frequent interference of governmental authorities, usually expressed in repressive edicts. Japan was subject to so many that Donald Shively asks rhetorically, "Why did they not abolish *kabuki* outright?" His answer: "The attitude of the *bakufu* [military government] seems to have been that *kabuki* was, like prostitution, a necessary evil. These were the two wheels of the vehicle of pleasure, useful to assuage the people and divert them from more serious mischief" (Shively 1955, 336).

Shively notes that antitheatrical laws passed in Edo were of three principal types: (1) those that segregated theatre people from ordinary society, (2) sumptuary edicts that maintained limits on the extravagance of lifestyles and stage productions in a society that could not condone actors showing greater luxury than what was appropriate to their low social class, and (3) regulations restricting dramatic themes to what would not threaten the political or social status quo. The latter included plays of too much sexual suggestiveness, although homosexual as well as heterosexual frankness still managed to figure in many plays. Shively reflects on but does not list restrictions on architectural arrangements, the use of candles, and building materials—most of which stemmed from fear of fire. (See the chapter on "The Development of the Physical Theatre" in Ernst 1974.)

Plays in both cultures were canceled for allegedly subversive materials but not in great numbers. This normally occurred in Japan after a play opened, there being no office comparable to the Lord Chamberlain's until 1875 to exercise prior restraint. *Kabuki* did not seek to criticize government so much as it sought to avoid crippling restrictions on the use of certain kinds of material. The theatre could not openly subvert official restrictions, but it managed to devise methods that—despite occasionally intense efforts at surveillance—allowed it to deal with restricted material with a limited degree of freedom. For instance, in 1644 the government issued the first of repeated edicts against the dramatization of events relating to the contemporary samurai class. This was emphatically reinforced in 1703 after the theatre began to introduce scenes inspired by the recent Asano family vendetta, in which forty-seven samurai faithfully avenged their lord, a story best known from its 1748 dramatization as *Kanadehon Chûshingura* (for translations, see Keene 1971 and Brandon 1982). *Kabuki* soon created a coded system in which certain times, places, and individuals from the past were substituted for individuals of present or recent times. The camouflage was usually so thin that the government had to have known that its rules were being violated, but as long as it recognized an effort being made to conform to its proscriptions, it was content to look the other way. There is widespread belief that the heroes of several tremendously popular, never repressed, plays like *Sukeroku* or *Shibaraku* were subversive figures whose dynamic victories over evil samurai represented wish fulfillment for townsmen oppressed by the warrior class.

In contrast to the three main grounds for Japanese censorship, Calhoun Winton presents five for the English theatre of the time. He lists (1) criticism of the government; (2) critical depictions of foreign allies, their rulers, or people; (3) "comment on religious controversy"; (4) blasphemous or profane language; and (5) satirical attacks on important persons (1980, 294). All these items could conceivably be conflated into Shively's third category (i.e., politically or socially offensive subject matter). Despite these restrictions, such transgressions were not absent from English drama. A number of plays, mainly the comedies, made fair game of actual political figures or of social groups—such as the anti–Charles I merchants or "cits" negatively portrayed in Restoration plays—who represented particular ideologies. As in Japan it was necessary, when skewering important figures, to disguise their actual personages. To defer legal action, periods and locales might also be altered, as in *Venice Preserv'd* (1682), but not always: John Gay's *The Beggar's Opera* (1728), which satirizes Robert Walpole, and *The Critic* (1779), which attacks Lord North, were set in contemporary England.

The existence in England of opposing political parties allowed for more freedom of thought in that country; in Japan there was one dictatorial "party," so opportunities were notably rarer. Regardless of the existence of an official English censorship, the office seems to have acted repressively only at certain times, most notably for several years after Walpole passed the Licensing Act of 1737 and in the closing years of the century, following the outbreak of the French Revolution. In both Japan and England, audiences, being largely conservative, were not seriously disturbed by overt censorship. Fear of being shut down was strong enough in both countries to prevent noticeable rule breaking, and theatre labored under the burden of a rigorous self-censorship, which many will agree is the worst kind.

One of the most oppressive restrictions in both England and Japan had to do with the number of theatres legally allowed to operate. In the early seventeenth century, although regulations existed, the right to run a theatre in Japan and England was relatively easy to obtain. There were far more theatres operating in London before the Commonwealth (1642) and in Edo-Osaka-Kyoto before the 1650s than afterwards. With the coming of the Restoration London was forced to get by with two royally approved theatres, the patent houses. For a time in the late seventeenth century, only one was operating. By the 1730s, after the rise and fall of several other venues, Londoners had ready access to four theatres: Goodman's Fields and the Little Theatre in the Hay were giving regular performances in addition to the licensed houses, the new Covent Garden (1732) and the old Drury Lane (1663). This number was halved again by the Licensing Act of 1737, allowing only Covent Garden and Drury Lane to produce plays, although they continually had to battle infringement by nonpatents (the "minors"), many of which continued to appear, finding one way or the other to circumvent the licensing laws. From then into the nineteenth century the patents held fast to their monopoly as the only legitimate, nonoperatic theatres allowed to produce both spoken drama and all sorts of musical and pantomimic genres, sharing their rights only with the Little Theatre in the Hay, which was granted a patent in the summer months from 1766. From 1766, then, London had three officially licensed theatres for (primarily) straight drama, although there were many "illegitimate" venues producing entertainments, some suppressed by the law and others protected by various ruses.

Each of Japan's theatre cities was also limited to a small number of officially licensed theatres. From the mid-1650s, following a brief period in which *kabuki* was banned (see below), there were four major theatres (*za*) in Edo: the Yamamura-za, founded in 1642; the Nakamura-za, founded in 1624; the Ichimura-za, founded in 1660; and the Morita-za, founded in 1663. In 1714, following the discovery that a lady-in-waiting at the shôgun's court had been dallying at the Yamamura-za with a handsome star, the parties to the affair were exiled and the theatre was liquidated, leaving only three licensed theatres, the so-called Edo *sanza* (Edo's "three theatres"), one or the other of which was occasionally replaced by an "alternate theatre" (*hikae yagura*)[4] when business was bad. The *sanza* restrictions were not lifted by official action until the early 1870s, whereas the equivalent English event occurred in 1843.

Japan had a host of minor playhouses (*koshibai* and *miyaji shibai*) in addition to the majors (*ôshibai*). These were low-price theatres granted temporary permission to produce plays on the grounds of shrines and temples (and elsewhere) during special, festival-related occasions. They were not unlike the profusion of lesser, often short-lived theatres (especially the fairground variety) that existed in London as a perpetual pain to the patents and whose numbers no one knows for sure. One recent estimate suggests that there may have been an average of about twenty theatres, major and minor, giving productions in each of the major Japanese cities of the period (see Torigoe 1997). The duration of permission was typically one hundred days of good weather, but ways were found to circumvent this rule. The majors were strictly confined to specific neighborhoods, but the minors could be anywhere in the city. Whereas their English equivalents were deprived of certain rights in their repertory, the Japanese minors were denied physical features, such as a draw curtain, that would have given them equal dignity with the majors. Still, they provided significant competition and on rare occasions produced actors who became stars at the majors, just as did Goodman's Fields when it gave David Garrick his first claim to fame. However, once a *kabuki* actor left the majors to play in the minors, he could not return. English actors had no such restrictions. Over and over the minors in England and Japan came back to life after being repressed by the authorities. The theatre workers of both countries were clever at getting around authority.

---

[4]The word *yagura* refers to the drum tower at the front of the theatre. It served as public acknowledgment of the theatre's licensed status.

Actors

One of the first things one learns about *kabuki* is that it is, and always has been, dominated by its actors. *Kabuki* plays were little more than vehicles for great stars, who freely adapted and revised the repertory to suit their personal tastes. Playwrights did not gain substantial authority until the nineteenth century and then only rarely. Likewise, as Marion Jones notes, London's theatre was emphatically nonliterary: "We should bear in mind that for the whole of this period the theatre in England was an actors' theatre. . . . Their [the actors'] professional objective was the display of each actor's person and techniques to the best advantage within the context of a given play's demands" (1976, 131–32).

In response to the outbreak of civil war in 1642, the Puritans in Parliament closed London's theatres. As Simon Trussler suggests, this was probably intended as a temporary move, but it led to what was—despite momentary flareups of activity—the cessation of theatre in London throughout the eighteen-year Commonwealth period (1994, 115). Ten years later, in 1652, the Tokugawa shôgunate banned *kabuki* because of brawls inspired by rivalries over the performers in the homosexual boys' *kabuki* (*wakashû kabuki*). In this case the ban lasted less than a year. When *kabuki* was reinstituted, however, it was with certain legal pressures, including a proscription against the word *kabuki* and a prohibition against the boys unless they abandoned their fashionable forelocks and shaved their heads in the less attractive adult male style. Official sanctions against using the stage as a marketplace for bedroom favors led to rapid developments in the art of acting as women, and roles for females became increasingly important and complex.

When Charles II was restored to the British throne in 1660, the London theatre was reestablished, but the pre-1642 practice of boys playing females was discarded. Thus just around the time that the art of female impersonation was being seriously advanced in Japan, the art of the actress was coming into its own in England. As has often been the case, governmental proscriptions were responsible for artistic revolutions.

Women, having been officially outlawed in Japanese theatre since 1629, could not reappear, so it fell to men to play their roles. In England women had never been legally barred but were prevented by convention from performing. The convention changed when the needs of the new, foreign-influenced drama and theatre were instituted under Charles II. Actresses appeared as a natural outgrowth of artistic developments in London, just as did the female impersonators of Japan. In each case there could have been no other step.

Cross-dressing had been a convention of *kabuki* from its early days for both sexes until the actresses were banned, but in post-Restoration England, for all its frequency, it was mainly restricted to women playing men in the popular "breeches" roles that allowed them to show off attractive figures normally hidden by ample dresses. An excuse could always be found: circumstances might force the character to disguise herself, which allowed for the inevitable "disguise penetrated" shock, or she might choose to do so as an expression of her free will, in one of the popular "roaring girl" roles. Occasionally, an actress actually played a male role, Peg Woffington as Sir Harry Wildair (originally written for a man) being a famous example. Nevertheless, apart from its earliest years, when pre-Restoration female impersonators like Edward Kynaston returned to the stage, the post-Restoration English theatre never exploited cross-dressing on a level anywhere near its Japanese counterpart.

The number of women in a typical British company was always about half the number of men. The *onnagata* were even more greatly outnumbered by actors of male roles. Whereas a Restoration company typically had twenty-five to thirty actors, an average figure for an English playhouse of the 1729–1747 period was seventy-four (Scouten 1968, cxxv). Two Edo theatres in 1769 had sixty-one actors, and the third had forty-nine (Hattori 1993, 83). Eight actors were strictly *onnagata* at one, five at another, and three at the third, so male role actors were obviously required to play female roles on frequent occasions. In the same year, an Edo company, including actors, resident dramatists, musicians, backstage and front-of-house personnel, came to 346 at one house, 323 at another, and 211 at the third (Hattori 1993, 85). On the other hand, "The two patent theatres . . . supported about three hundred actors, actresses, dancers, singers, musicians, house servants and itinerant troupers" (Stone 1968, lxxxvii). *Kabuki* thus had a smaller acting company but a much larger group of nonperforming employees. English actors were hired by specific theatres for varying periods—brief during the Restoration, but later three years became common. Japanese players were contracted for only one season at a time and, except for emergencies (as when their theatre burned down), could not act for another company until their term was up.

Great versatility was expected of actors in both England and Japan. Specialization was also prevalent among actors of both traditions. As a consequence, many roles were specifically written with particular Japanese or English players in mind. Sometimes such roles became associated with an actor for life. English actors had far more roles in their standard repertory than did Japanese thespians because their bills changed more frequently. Drury Lane produced seventy plays during the 1721–1722 season; John Mills played fifty roles that season (Avery and Scouten

1968, cxxviii)! A more standard figure was about fifteen roles a season. This was closer to what most leading Japanese actors could expect to play annually, as they appeared in only five or six plays, which, lasting from dawn to dusk, often saw them handling two or three roles in what English actors called "doubling." Many *kabuki* roles, in fact, were written to reveal widely contrasting qualities, as Jekyll and Hyde–like characters often waited in disguise to reveal their true natures. A single role, then, was often the equivalent of two roles, and to it an actor might add other roles as well. Doubling was not uncommon in England, but it fell out of favor as the companies expanded.

The social position of actors in both nations was very low, despite their fame and, in some cases, wealth. In Japan they were "riverbed beggars" (*kawara kojiki*), among other slurs, and in England they were legally tagged as "rogues, vagabonds, sturdy beggars, and vagrants." Gradually, the dignified reputations of various actors began to elevate the profession. Some English actors were able to join exclusive clubs, and some *kabuki* stars became recognized participants in respected social and literary circles. In both cultures the profession of acting was open to anyone with the talent and will. *Kabuki* had so many families in the early seventeenth century that no actor of worth was likely to be turned away, but as the years passed it became increasingly difficult to break in without a strong family connection, even if by adoption. English actors, too, could find the path to success strewn with hardship, as Philip H. Highfill, Jr., writes: "There were only a few ways for aspirants to gain the boards of the London patent theatres. A youth of talent could be born into a family connected to a London theatre and obtain preferential treatment and early training" (1980, 153). The next-best thing was to obtain an important actor or manager as a patron, which is not terribly different from the custom of being adopted or taken in as an apprentice by the equivalent person in Japan. Some English actors were able to gain attention at provincial or minor London theatres (Garrick did both), and Nakamura Utaemon I (1714–1791), son of a rural physician, became a big star in the city only after gaining valuable experience as a strolling player (Nomura 1988, 204).

The highly conventionalized nature of *kabuki* acting meant that young actors had to learn—as they still do—in a strict master-apprenticeship system instituted early in *kabuki*'s history. Ichikawa Danjûrô V (1741–1806) went beyond the system by establishing actor-training workshops and allowing even nondisciples to participate. No comparable training workshops evolved for contemporary British actors, and sporadic attempts to found schools or "nurseries" were abortive. Actors did learn the standard roles via a method like that of the Japanese, at least until the mid–eighteenth century. As Jones writes: "In practice, the best way to be sure of pleasing in any established role was to play it as exactly like its acknowledged master as possible" (1976, 142). Despite the power of convention in the acting of famous parts, actors occasionally offered revolutionary interpretations, such as Charles Macklin's Shylock in 1741 and Nakamura Nakazô I's radical version of Sadakurô that startled audiences in the 1766 revival of *Chûshingura*.

In London not only were aristocrats allowed in the playhouses, but many enjoyed interacting with the players. Some noblemen even had pretensions to acting talent, and instances are known where they might rent a theatre to display their skills. In Japan, the samurai class was legally barred from going to *kabuki*. Nevertheless, many of them were so inordinately fond of theatricals that they attended in disguise. Records prove that, from the mid–eighteenth century, this fondness extended to avid studying of *kabuki* vocal and musical skills and giving amateur performances of *kabuki* dramas in their homes, a practice deemed so inappropriate to their station that it was officially repressed during the Kansei reforms of the 1790s (Kominz 1993, 67).

There were few restrictions on romantic or marital relations between English players and the upper classes, but, as the previously cited scandal concerning the court lady and *kabuki* star attests, such freedom was not allowed in Japan. There was, though, considerable dalliance—homosexual as well as heterosexual—between actors and the townman class.

Acting dynasties were known in England, as witness such names as Kemble and Hallam. Their numbers and artistic significance, however, were dwarfed by the theatre families of Japan, where the Ichikawas, Nakamuras, Onoes, and others continue to thrive.

Actors of eighteenth-century England and Japan were increasingly subject to the kind of public fascination with their offstage lives we find today in our tabloids and TV shows. Publication of biographical and autobiographical writings and of anecdotal commentaries revealed their private lives to their fans. Gossip about actors was devoured ravenously by English and Japanese fans. Serious writings on acting also appeared. Japan, for example, produced such famous actor commentaries (*geidan*) as the *Yakusha Rongo* (Actors' Analects) (see Torigoe and Dunn 1969); and Nakamura Nakazô I's two-volume autobiography reminds one of such memoirs as those of Anne Oldfield and David Garrick. The annual actors' critiques (*yakusha hyôbanki*) were another source of personal as well as artistic commentary (see "Yakusha Hyôbanki" in Leiter 1997a). In addition, each actor was given a precise ranking, something no English actor of the day had to tolerate.

A popular top-ranked *kabuki* actor could earn a fortune. Ichikawa

Danjûrô II received the highest annual salary of the century, estimated at what today might equal half a million dollars. Although the leading English actors made comfortable livings, not even the best paid of them could command anything like this sum. On the other hand, those few who, like Garrick, combined successful managerial careers with acting could retire in considerable comfort. In England actors were paid only for those days on which they performed, but *kabuki* actors seem not to have faced this problem. Actors in both nations are known to have supplemented their incomes with outside businesses, and *kabuki* actors were also able to earn handsome sums by endorsing commercial products.

Each country had an active provincial touring system, with clearly defined "circuits," during the eighteenth century, and the actors experienced similarly harsh conditions. The provinces were deemed a good training ground for future success in the big cities. Major stars sometimes earned substantial sums by playing with touring companies during the summer seasons. The English actors were hired according to their specialties or "lines of business," a loose equivalent to the Japanese players' system of "role types" (*yakugara*). After gaining official approval to perform, the actors would announce their arrival in a new Japanese or English town by marching through the streets, accompanied by a drummer. Actors in both cultures had to put up not only with rascally managers but with rowdy audiences who would talk back to the dramatic characters and sometimes even mistake stage events for the real thing. (See Nishiyama 1997 for details on Japan's strolling actors, and Rosenfeld 1970 for background on British strollers.)

Theatrical Architecture, Scenic Methods, and Lighting

When the Restoration began, the only remaining unroofed London theatre was the soon-to-be-disused Red Bull. *Kabuki* theatres, however, remained either completely or partially unroofed until 1723 (Shively 1978, 15). English and Japanese theatres had more than roofs in common. Both were equipped with elevator traps, for example. England's traps evolved much earlier than Japan's, going back to the Middle Ages, and they apparently were included in early Restoration theatres. According to Gunji Masakatsu, inconclusive evidence suggests that there may have been pre-elevator *kabuki* traps in 1683, 1694, and 1699, with the first elevator version possibly appearing in 1700 (Gunji 1970, 11–12). Most other sources, though, suggest later dates. Elevator traps capable of moving "People, properties, machines, and scenes" (Visser 1980, 94) were common in eighteenth-century London and operated on principles akin to *kabuki*'s. The *kabuki* elevator allowed supernatural figures to appear on its smaller trap, but, with one or two exceptions, reserved use of its trap on the auditorium runway (*hanamichi*) for magical figures or spirits. On the London stage, which had no *hanamichi*, traps were traditionally the province of "ghosts, demons, allegorical figures, or gods" (Visser 1980, 96). Thunder or lightning effects hid the sound of the elevator in England, whereas in Edo—where conventionalized musical passages usually stood in for more literal sound effects—eerie drumbeats suggesting thunder or wind did the same. English and Japanese traps could also serve for any space that had to be lower than the stage locale, such as cellars, wells, bodies of water, and the like. Elaborate devices rose from underneath in both countries, and, although *kabuki* is renowned for its ability to raise entire multistory sets by these means, the eighteenth-century English stage could perform wonders of its own.

Playhouse architecture in Japan and England shared many similarities. Theatres of the 1730s in both countries were essentially rectangular spaces, although the corners of the English rectangles were rounded. Interiors were somewhat differently arranged, and *kabuki* had the unique feature of one, and later, two *hanamichi*. But English and Japanese theatres were fundamentally similar in being laid out in a box, pit, and gallery plan (see Leiter 1997b for pictures and diagrams of an extant Edo-period theatre). Of course, Japanese audiences sat on the floor and British spectators used chairs. The auditorium floors in both were raked. Moreover, the *hanamichi* was only occasionally a part of *kabuki* playhouses of the day and was not permanently installed until the 1740s (see "Hanamichi no Tanjô" in Suwa 1991). In addition, British and Japanese theatres did not differ greatly in size during the first half of the eighteenth century, when capacity was around one thousand. England's theatres eventually expanded in much greater increments, especially after the 1790s renovations to Drury Lane and Covent Garden, which made them gargantuan in comparison not only to their earlier forms but to contemporary *kabuki* theatres as well. The largest *kabuki* houses appear to have held about fifteen hundred by the century's end, when London's held over three thousand. Raz reminds us that *kabuki* theatres could pack as many people in for a hit as possible and that one record speaks of the incredible sum of five or six thousand crammed into a theatre in Nara, while another one thousand milled around outside, unable to enter (Raz 1983, 173).

Actor-audience intimacy in *kabuki* and English theatre was further intensified by the important adjunct of an apron allowing those in the pit to surround downstage action on three sides. This extension, called the *tsuke butai* (literally, "connected stage"), was added in the late seventeenth century and lasted in most theatres into the nineteenth. The British forestage was whittled away sooner, but its side doors lasted until the 1820s. A slight difference between English and Japanese forestages is that the latter allowed small areas of pit space on either of its sides, between the stage and the side boxes, whereas the English forestage ran smack into the side boxes.

During the eighteenth century the proscenium arch was one prominent architectural feature found in the English theatre and not in the Japanese. Nevertheless, a singular Japanese element served to frame much of the action upstage of the apron until its removal in 1796. This was the stage roof supported by onstage pillars, derived from the *nô* theatre. With its removal a framing arrangement similar to the proscenium was effected by the overhead cloth border (*ichimonji*), but the general impression was similar to that of a contemporary endstage. English stages were masked overhead by a more elaborate system of borders, usually designed to match the side scenes and shutters and confined in most cases to sky, tree, and architectural features. *Kabuki* employed a variety of decorative borders at the front, either of colorful curtains or of hanging branches (*tsurieda*) dressed with seasonal flora.

England and Japan were both preoccupied with the development of ever more illusionistic scenery and special effects. Scene shifting that allowed sets to be transformed from one reality to another before the spectators' eyes was a goal of both *kabuki* and the English stages, both of which painted much of their scenery on flats. *Kabuki* had devices for rapid shifts that would not have been out of place at Drury Lane or Covent Garden. In fact, a British scenic transformation device, the "Falling Flaps" method, is the same as *kabuki*'s *aorigaeshi* (or *uchi-gaeshi*). Noting that the device goes back to at least 1743, Richard Southern quotes an 1803 account that describes "those double flat scenes, which are also used to produce instantaneous changes. The whole scene being covered with pieces of canvas, framed and moving upon hinges, one side [of each of these hinged flaps] is painted to represent a certain scene, and the other to represent one totally different" (Southern 1960, 800). The flaps were raised and showed their obverse sides to the spectators; when a catch was removed, gravity caused them to fall, revealing their reverse side and creating an altogether different picture. The comparable *kabuki* method was invented by playwright Kanai Sanshô (1731–1797). A description of the method tells us that "a painted flat . . . is built with a separate section attached to its center by hinges. When the extra section is moved from one side to the other, like a page in a book, a new painted surface is revealed" (Leiter 1997a, 16).

Flying, too, was known in both England and Japan. Eighteenth-century English flying was usually by means of "machines" that allowed individuals or groups to descend to the stage or rise to the flies, with the possibility of up-and-down or horizontal movement. *Kabuki,* which introduced flying (*chûnori*) toward the end of the eighteenth century, preferred to fly individual actors across the stage or over the heads of the spectators on a wire or rope. Numerous other such effects were shared by England and Japan, including the use of onstage water tanks, small models for *trompe l'oeil* perspective, and pyrotechnics.

Although both Japan and England depended for many years on stock scenic units, scenery became increasingly local and play-specific as time passed. Scene painting techniques were highly sophisticated in both traditions. Some *kabuki* scenery, like the river flowing toward the audience in *Imoseyama Onna Teikin,* even employed perspective effects, although *kabuki* had no raked stage. Western perspective was being imported at the time by Japanese print artists, so the only surprise here is that the stage did not make even more use of it. There is also an extraordinary resemblance between the two nations' means of producing the flowing water effect, that is, contiguous large rollers painted with waves and with handles at either end rotated by stagehands.

The chief source of *kabuki* lighting from the 1720s or 1730s was actually from removable sliding windows (*madobuta* or *akari mado*) high up over the left and right galleries (*sajiki*), where theatre workers manipulated the amount of daylight streaming in. Early Restoration performances, staged during the daytime, also employed natural light available from playhouse windows or from the cupola. Decorative paper lanterns (*bazuri chôchin*) adorned with actors' names were introduced in the 1760s. Illuminated by candles (oil was considered too dangerous), they hung from the ceiling and side galleries but offered minimal illumination, certainly nothing like what was provided by the chandeliers over the English pit. But *kabuki* did have a novel way of lighting an actor's face when necessary. In scenes requiring a feeling of mystery, the overhead shutters would be closed, darkening the house, and stage assistants would hold long, flexible bamboo poles (*sashidashi*), with upright candles fitted to their ends, before the actor's face, thereby spotlighting him. By the late eighteenth century, however, England was making far more rapid technological progress in lighting than was Japan.

The eighteenth-century English theatre used footlights (either candles or oil) from the time of the Restoration. *Kabuki*'s candle footlights (*izaribi* or *sashikomi*) first came into use toward the end of the eighteenth century. The candles were attached to squared-off poles that sat in holders affixed to the front of the stage, their flames rising a foot and a half to two feet higher than the stage floor. These holders are invariably seen in woodblock prints of theatre interiors from the late eighteenth century on. Because of frequent proscriptions against open flames, small metal hand lanterns (*kantera*) came into use in the 1780s for local illumination. Theatres in Japan constantly burned down, their average life being ten years, whereas only two major conflagrations consumed London theatres during our period.

It is instructive to compare the sizes of London's theatres with Edo's, although some of the figures given are conjectural. From 1732 to 1782—when it held fourteen hundred—Covent Garden's exterior dimensions were a width of 62′ by a depth of 117′, and Drury Lane's exterior proportions from 1674 to 1775—when it at first held from five hundred to one thousand, and then from eighteen hundred to twenty-three hundred—were 58′ or 59′ by 114′. The Nakamura-za in the 1690s was 71′ by 97.5′. Thus *kabuki* theatres, or this typical one at any rate, were originally wider but less deep than the major English examples. However, late-eighteenth-century renovations saw the English playhouses grow considerably larger. Covent Garden after 1792 was approximately 62′ by 180′ and seated 3,000, and Drury Lane after 1794 was 86′ by 204′ and held 3,611. The Nakamura-za never was larger than in 1809, when it measured 80′ by 138.5′ and held about twelve hundred. (English figures cited here are from Langhans 1980, 61–62; Japanese figures are from Shively 1978, 14.) Apart from the great depth of the 1794 Drury Lane, the principal London and Edo playhouses were not very different in exterior proportions, but the interior arrangements of the English playhouse included several tiers of boxes whereas only two tiers were permitted in Japan. Thus far more audience members could attend a London playhouse than one in Edo.

The curtain first became a major feature of the London stage in the early Restoration, just about the time that it was introduced into *kabuki*. Curtains are a relative rarity in Asian theatre, but *kabuki* practically makes a fetish of them. At first sight the use of the curtains in Japan and England looks similar, but there are significant differences. London's curtain long remained a green "French valance," which rose in festoons, whereas the standard *kabuki* curtain was (and remains) a traveler in vertical stripes, the most familiar colors being the now ubiquitous green, persimmon, and black. This curtain was (and is) run on and off by a stage assistant, whose timing contributes significantly to the opening or closing mood. Apart from occasional exceptions, the English curtain rose after the prologue and descended at the end of the play, so, with most scene changes done in full view, and with established conventions to indicate the ends of scenes and acts—such as actors exiting after reciting a couplet—its presence was not necessarily a factor in dramatic structure. In Japan, however, the curtain was invented in 1664, at the same time as the advent of multiact dramas, and became very useful as a way to mark the passage of time or shifts in locale. The presence of the curtain surely helped *kabuki* develop changeable scenery, which, like the advent of the *onnagata*'s art, made the theatre more realistic. (For a summary of English curtain usage see Visser 1980, 61– 62; for *kabuki* curtains see "Maku" in Leiter 1997a, 384–85.) In fact, eighteenth-century critic John Dennis's remark that the Restoration's patentees "alterd all at once the whole Face of the stage by introducing scenes and Women, which added probability to the Dramatick Actions and made evry thing look more naturally" (quoted in Southern 1976, 120–21) could be—with *onnagata* substituted for "Women"—equally descriptive of *kabuki* in the 1660s. The English stage enjoyed the advantage of wing and groove shifting, which could look magical when well done. This occurred before *kabuki* created its methods of shifting sets by sliding and revolving stages; it therefore needed to hide the changes. The technological advances of wagons and disks, so crucial to eighteenth-century *kabuki* history, would remain absent from England until the twentieth century.

Conclusion

Many more comparisons could be made between the English and Japanese stages of the years considered here, and everything that has been addressed is open to further discussion. Clearly, it would be difficult if not impossible to find outside of the West so many features in any one form that resemble, as do *kabuki*'s, those of the English stage of the same time. I believe that seeing *kabuki* in the light of contemporary Western practices helps not only to illuminate this theatre form itself but to shed light on the non-Japanese theatre as well.

Works Cited

Japanese names are referenced in Japanese fashion, family name first without a comma before the given name.
Avery, Emmet L., and Arthur Scouten. 1968. *The London Stage, 1660–1700: A Critical Introduction*. Carbondale: Southern Illinois University Press.
Brandon, James R., ed. 1982. *Chūshingura: Studies in the Puppet Theatre*. Honolulu: University of Hawaii Press.
Brandon, James R., William P. Malm, and Donald Shively, eds. 1978. *Studies in*

Kabuki: Its Acting, Music, and Historical Context. Honolulu: University of Hawaii Press.

Ernst, Earle. 1974. *The Kabuki Theatre.* 2d ed. Honolulu: University of Hawaii Press.

Fujita Minoru, and Leonard Pronko, eds. 1996. *Shakespeare East and West.* New York: St. Martin's Press.

Gunji Masakatsu. 1969. *Kabuki.* Trans. John Bester. Palo Alto, Calif.: Kodansha.

———. 1970. *Kabuki Bukuro* (*Kabuki* Bag). Tokyo: Seiabô.

Hattori Yukio. 1993. *Edo Kabuki* (*Kabuki* in Edo). Tokyo: Iwanami Shoten.

Highfill, Philip H., Jr. 1980. "Performers and Performing." In *The London Theatre World: 1660–1800,* ed. Robert D. Hume. Carbondale: Southern Illinois University Press.

Hume, Robert D., ed. 1980. *The London Theatre World: 1660–1800.* Carbondale: Southern Illinois University Press.

Ihara Toshirô, ed. 1956–63. *Kabuki Nenpyô* (*Kabuki* Chronology). 8 vols. Tokyo: Iwanami Shoten.

Jones, Marion. 1976. "Actors and Repertory." In *The Revels History of Drama in English.* Vol. 5, *1660–1750,* ed. John Loftis, Richard Southern, Marion Jones, and A. H. Scouten. London: Methuen.

Kanasawa Yasutaka. 1972. *Ichikawa Danjûrô.* Tokyo: Seibô.

Keene, Donald. 1971. *Chûshingura: The Treasury of Loyal Retainers.* New York: Columbia University Press.

Kominz, Laurence. 1993. "Ichikawa Danjûrô V and *Kabuki*'s Golden Age." In *The Floating World Revisited,* ed. Donald Jenkins. Honolulu: Portland Museum and University of Hawaii Press.

Langhans, Edward. 1980. "The Theatres." In *The London Theatre World: 1660–1800,* ed. Robert D. Hume. Carbondale: Southern Illinois University Press.

Leiter, Samuel L. 1997a. *New Kabuki Encyclopedia: A Revised Adaptation of Kabuki Jiten.* Westport, Conn.: Greenwood Press.

———. 1997b. "The Kanamaru-za: Japan's Oldest *Kabuki* Theatre." *Asian Theatre Journal* 14, no. 2 (spring): 56–92.

The London Stage: A Critical Introduction. 1968. 5 vols. Carbondale: Southern Illinois University Press.

Milhous, Judith. 1980. "Company Management." In *The London Theatre World: 1660–1800,* ed. Robert D. Hume. Carbondale: Southern Illinois University Press.

Nishiyama Matsunosuke. 1997. *Edo Culture: Daily Life and Diversions in Urban Japan, 1600–1868.* Trans. and ed. Gerald Groemer. Honolulu: University of Hawaii Press.

Nomura Jusaburô. 1988. *Kabuki Jinmei Jiten* (Biographical Dictionary of *Kabuki*). Tokyo: Nichigai.

Pronko, Leonard. 1967. "*Kabuki* and the Elizabethan Theatre." *Educational Theatre Journal* 19 (March): 9–16.

———. 1994. "Creating *Kabuki* for the West." In *Japanese Theatre for the West,* ed. Akemi Horie-Webber. Special issue of *Contemporary Theatre Review* 1 (part 2): 113–22.

Raz, Jacob. 1983. *Audiences and Actors: A Study of Their Interaction in Traditional Japanese Theatre.* Leiden: Brill.

Rosenfeld, Sybil. [1939] 1970. *Strolling Players and Drama in the Provinces.* Cambridge: Cambridge University Press.

Scouten, Arthur H. 1968. *The London Stage, 1729–1747: A Critical Introduction.* Carbondale: Southern Illinois University Press.

Shively, Donald. 1955. "*Bakufu* versus *Kabuki.*" *Harvard Journal of Asiatic Studies* 18 (December): 326–56.

———. 1978. "The Social Environment of *Tokugawa Kabuki.*" In *Studies in Kabuki: Its Acting, Music, and Historical Context,* ed. James R. Brandon, William P. Malm, and Donald Shively. Honolulu: University of Hawaii Press.

Southern, Richard. 1960. "Trickwork on the English Stage." In *Oxford Companion to the Theatre,* 2d ed., ed. Phyllis Hartnoll. London: Oxford University Press.

———. 1976. "Theatres and Scenery." In *The Revels History of Drama in English.* Vol. 5, *1660–1750,* ed. John Loftis, Richard Southern, Marion Jones, and A. H. Scouten. London: Methuen.

Stone, George Winchester, Jr. 1968. *The London Stage, 1747–1776: A Critical Introduction.* Carbondale: Southern Illinois University Press.

Suwa Haruo. 1991. *Kabuki no Hôhô* (*Kabuki* Methods). Tokyo: Benseisha.

Torigoe Bunzô. 1997. "*Kabuki:* The Actors' Theatre." Trans. and adapted by James R. Brandon. In *Japanese Theatre in the World,* ed. Samuel L. Leiter. New York: Japan Society.

Torigoe Bunzô, and Charles Dunn, trans. and commentators. 1969. *The Actors' Analects.* Tokyo: Tokyo University Press.

Trussler, Simon. 1994. *The Cambridge Illustrated History of the British Theatre.* Cambridge: Cambridge University Press.

Tsubouchi Shôyô. 1960. "Chikamatsu's Resemblance to Shakespeare." In Tsubouchi Shôyô and Yamamoto Jirô, *History and Characteristics of Kabuki,* trans. and ed. Ryôzô Matsumoto. Yokohama: Yamagata Heiji.

Visser, Colin. 1980. "Scenery and Technical Design." In *The London Theatre World: 1660–1800,* ed. Robert D. Hume. Carbondale: Southern Illinois University Press.

Waterhouse, David. 1981. "Actors, Artists and the Stage in Eighteenth-Century England." In *Theatre in the Eighteenth Century,* ed. J. R. Browning. New York and London: Garland.

Winton, Calhoun. 1980. "Dramatic Censorship." In *The London Theatre World: 1660–1800,* ed. Robert D. Hume. Carbondale: Southern Illinois University Press.

Yamazaki Masakazu. 1994. *Individualism and the Japanese: An Alternative Approach to Cultural Comparison.* Trans. Barbara Sugihara. Tokyo: Japan Echo.

Boys, Women, or

Phantasmal Androgynes?

Elizabethan and *Kabuki* Female Representation

Leonard C. Pronko

*A*LMOST A CENTURY AGO, an American actress speaking of the most popular playwright of the day, Clyde Fitch, in his role as a director and model of female roles, claimed, "Not a woman of us could approach him in look, manner, and, above all, voice" (quoted in Schmidgall 1994, 442). About a century earlier, in 1787, Goethe saw a performance of Goldoni's *The Mistress of the Inn* in Rome, where women were still excluded from the stage. He declared himself won over by the young man playing Mirandolina and felt a pleasure he had not felt before (Ferris 1993, 49). Going back another hundred years, we find several memorialists of the Restoration expressing a similar delight in the feminine charms of a male actor, Edward Kynaston. John Downes, who must have seen him frequently and at very close range (for he was the prompter in Betterton's and Davenant's companies), wrote that when he was very young Kynaston "made a Compleat Female Stage Beauty, performing his parts so well . . . that it has since been Disputable among the Judicious, whether any Woman that succeeded him so Sensibly touch'd the Audience as he" (quoted in Bentley 1984, 115). Pepys, in his diary entry for 7 January 1661, when Kynaston was twenty, notes that he "was clearly the prettiest woman in the whole house" (1970, 2:7). As we reach further into the past, arriving at the Caroline, Jacobean, and Elizabethan eras, we naturally find many more allusions to the success with which young men or boys impersonated women. Stephen Hammerton, who was famous for his handsome young male roles from 1638 to 1642, "was at first a most noted and beautiful Woman Actor" (Bentley 1984, 226). John Rice, who performed major women's parts in Shakespeare's troupe from 1607 to 1611, was known as "very fayre and beautiful"; he and Burbage were described in 1610 as "two absolute actors even the verie best our instant time can yield" (Bartholomeusz 1969, 11), surely high praise and lofty company for any actor. And eight years earlier, when the boy actor Salmon Pavy died at the age of thirteen, Ben Jonson called him "the stage's jewel" (Bentley 1984, 115), high tribute indeed for one who died so young.

If I have spent so long cataloging references to the beauty and skills of female impersonators, it is to remind us that there was until quite recently a long tradition of such acting even in the West. When we think of young men in women's roles today, we usually think of wild drag and high camp, but it has not always been so. These references to female impersonators as recently as the early twentieth century remind us that men-as-women could at one time be taken seriously as artists and indeed were frequently convincing and moving.

This may point to a long tradition, but it is certainly a choppy one and one that was frequently interrupted as women stepped into the breach, or men were briefly reinstated for religious or moral reasons. What seems missing is the result of so long a tradition: a true school of female impersonation, a vocabulary, a set of technical patterns and manners passed on from generation to generation. How could that be possible once the tradition had been lost during the Interregnum and men only occasionally played women's roles thereafter in England or in Europe generally? Custom, religion, or politics intervened, and the continuity of boys as women could be found only in the nonprofessional theatricals of schools.

Where the tradition persists, of course, is in the East, for all the major traditional forms of theatre in India, Southeast Asia, China, and Japan have highly developed arts of female impersonation. I would like to place this tradition, and particularly that of the *onnagata* of *kabuki*, side by side with the tradition, or rather the nontradition, of female impersonation in the West, particularly that of the boy actors of the English Renaissance, in order to see if we can understand anything new about the boy actors.

A number of scholars have pointed out striking similarities between Elizabethan-Jacobean theatre and traditional Asian theatres. Several have written more specifically of points of resemblance between Elizabethan and *kabuki* and in some cases have experimented with performances drawing on *kabuki* techniques to theatricalize the performance of these Western plays—plays that are most often presented today by actors and directors so stifled by television and film acting, or by the dominant mode of realism in the theatre (and the dominant mode of Stanislavski—or, what is worse, Strasberg—based training), that they scarcely realize that what they are performing is a dwarf version of Shakespeare, Jonson, Marlowe, Webster, or Middleton, deflated and flattened to the aesthetic of banality that seems to dominate so much of our art today. To "kabukify" these dramas is to seek once more the high theatricality, the virtuosity, that must have been an important part of Elizabethan and Jacobean acting and combine it with the flavorful sense of reality that is as much a part of *kabuki* as it is of Renaissance drama.

Experiments in such cross-cultural performances suggest that we still have much to learn but that the route is a very fruitful one. In my own experience the male roles have always been an easier transfer than the female ones: the style and techniques of *kabuki*'s *tachiyaku*, or performer of male roles, adapt readily to heroic characters of Shakespeare and Marlowe. But the vocal and movement patterns of the *onnagata* often appear to be too culture-specific to be easily adapted to women like Cordelia, Beatrice, Joanna, or the Duchess of Malfi. Just what is the relationship of the art of the boy actor to that of the *onnagata*?

We might reasonably expect large areas of similarity because both are arts of female impersonation or, if you prefer, arts that create the feminine, whether we agree that feminine is truly woman or is a creation of something that never existed, a purely artistic essentializing of woman. But England and Japan, even if we look at them both in the seventeenth century, are such distant and distinctive cultures that we should not be surprised to find profound differences.

The craft, as opposed to the art, of female impersonation, was imposed upon *kabuki* performers after 1629, when women were excluded from public presentations in Japan. Their roles were taken at first by young boys who in many cases had begun their careers as catamites. After 1653 mature men took on the roles and necessarily developed techniques to suggest qualities the audience would associate with women. It was at the end of the century that the first great *onnagata*, Yoshizawa Ayame, created what may be called the art of the *onnagata*. He advised behaving as a woman offstage as well as on and claimed that a female impersonator who even thought of becoming an actor of male roles could not be a good *onnagata*. In its long history *kabuki* has seen many great actors of these roles, and they developed increasingly rich and complex approaches to parts that display a dazzling range of character types and styles of performance. Two types that have long been considered quintessential *onnagata* roles are the princess and the elegant, high-ranking courtesan known as the *keisei*.

Despite Ayame's advice, a number of great actors have performed both *onnagata* and *tachiyaku* roles with success. A great *onnagata* today is no longer expected to live as a woman, although there are, of course, actors who continue that tradition in a somewhat attenuated form, probably as much from personal inclination as from artistic conviction. But there are others who are known for such "manly" hobbies as baseball and other sports, or even womanizing. What all *onnagata* share, however, is their mastery of a codified style of acting that has been refined over the centuries. The code allows them to present a female figure that, it is usually agreed, creates a woman more feminine than any woman ever seen on earth—more feminine but not necessarily more sexy, although many *kabuki* fans would argue for sexiness as well. Clearly the *onnagata* has no fleshly wares to display, but the equally attractive, more secret sexiness offered by some *onnagata* is suggested by a writer in the *Yakusha Mai Ogi,* an actors' critique from 1704, who says of the peerless Yoshizawa Ayame, "Even I do not know what is underneath his loincloth" (Laderriere 1984, 235).

Taking its point of departure in reality, but striving to find the beauty of pattern in both movement and speech, the highly stylized *onnagata* performance of the great princess and *keisei* roles lies at the antipodes of realistic representation. It may, indeed, be called the height of artifice, but at the same time it derives its patterns from real-life conditions. Unlike realism/naturalism, however, it refuses to hide those patterns, accentuating them for aesthetic or dramatic purposes.

Can this art compare in any way with that of the Elizabethan boy actors? First of all, we must admit that we know virtually nothing of the art of the boy actors. But what can we surmise from the few facts and references we do have? I would like to divide this brief discussion into three parts: the conditions under which the boys performed as women, the sexuality or sensuality of roles and actors, and paradigms of the feminine on which they might have drawn.

What I am calling conditions strike me as radically different: whereas the *onnagata,* since the time of Ayame in the early eighteenth century, would commit to a lifetime (often a long lifetime) of performing almost exclusively in female roles, the boy actor was expected to change over to male roles when he grew a beard and lost his childish voice. Most authorities agree that the boys performed from about the age of thirteen and that most of them had stopped playing women's roles by the time they were seventeen or eighteen. Twenty-one, in one case, seems to have been the absolute limit (Gurr 1992, 95; King 1992, 270). It is not even known whether many of them remained in acting troupes after their years of puberty. A dissenting voice is that of Peter Hyland who, following the pioneering research of Thomas W. Baldwin, suggests that such a role as Cleopatra, Lady Macbeth, or Gertrude was played by "a mature man and experienced actor" (Hyland 1987, 2).

This is an appealing hypothesis because it would help to explain the high praise given the men who played some of the women's roles. But the history of the boy actors is almost as brief as their individual careers, for unlike the *onnagata* they did not participate in a centuries-old tradition that allowed them to continue developing and deepening their art. Nor was the art passed on in families, from father to son, as it was in *kabuki*. Instead, for the less than a century that they acted professionally, the boy actors seem to have depended not on a laboriously acquired fund of coded behavior but on their natural charm, voice, and youthful freshness. *Natural* charm: because they stopped performing women's roles when their voices changed or they grew taller, it seems a plausible assumption that their performances were based on what we might call the "natural" femininity of a young boy—the higher voice, lower stature, and beardless face of a boy whose secondary sexual characterics had not yet developed. It also seems plausible that they made little attempt to use any of the artifices that the *onnagata* uses to create femininity. A brilliantly creative young actor may have occasionally invented, for example, a vocal technique for one role that would include playing on the break in the voice (*if* his voice had a break yet to play on) to suggest the androgynous character of a particularly strong woman, but such a technique (allegedly compared by Michener to the grating of a rusty hinge) would not have been universally accepted and passed on from master to student. By and large the boy actors, unlike the *onnagata,* did not have to devise ways of representing femininity because they were performing before "manhood" was upon them. They grew up in a culture that, some recent historians believe, assigned no clear gender roles to children: for example, male *and* female children in the Elizabethan era were dressed in skirts until the age of seven or so (Orgel 1989, 13). Just a few years out of their children's skirts, the boys may have been plunged into training and perhaps rehearsal skirts for the female roles they were expected to undertake.

To say that the boys were more natural and the *onnagata* more artful is not to deny the artistic achievements of the boys. The tradition was a long one, having begun in the schools, where it has continued well into the twentieth century (most of us can remember the striking photograph of Olivier as Katrina or pictures of Clyde Fitch or other young men playing women's roles at Amherst or other colleges and universities). By the time Shakespeare was writing, the young boys had already some reputation, and if Michael Goldman is right when he claims that "the powers of the actor determine the playwright's art" (Schmidgall 1990, 205), those powers must have been impressive to allow roles like Cleopatra and the Duchess of Malfi, the performance of which by thirteen- or fourteen-year-olds simply staggers the imagination. And yet, Shakespeare is so confident of the skill of his actor that he allows Cleopatra to express her fear that, if she is led back to Rome, she will see "some squeaking Cleopatra boy my greatness i' the posture of a whore" (5.2.216–17). That the boy dares remind the audience in this anguished moment that he too is a boy underneath his regal robes, knowing full well that he has the art to make them forget it immediately, indicates an extremely sophisticated degree of acting and understanding of the complexity of the actor's art—and indeed of the spectator's role as well.

Shakespeare's audience, like the *kabuki* audience, not yet exposed to the naturalistic heresy of the fourth wall, enjoyed both the virtuosity of the actor and the reality of the fictional situation. It is perfectly possible to weep with emotion and admire the artist at the same time—we do it often at the opera. Gary Schmidgall, in his brilliant analysis of *Shakespeare and Opera,* calls it "the Gemini factor": "the inescapable twinning of the role and the performer. . . . Consistency of effect," he writes, "is out of the question, because the two dramaturgies are magnificently *in*consistent and *un*natural in their pressure on the performers to run the gamut from utterly prosaic normalcy to the heights of purple-patched blank verse and coloratura fireworks" (193).

It is just possible that the boy actors were, like the *kabuki onnagata,* highly skilled artists, capable of flights of virtuosity and bravura acting on the one hand and of the utmost realism on the other—as were the better of their elders who were, of course, also their trainers. Both *kabuki* and Elizabethan performers were presentational actors who appeared quite natural at times and quite outrageous at others, but if they were good actors, they commanded their spectators' attention and emotion to such a degree that they became moving, true, real, and exciting. They certainly embodied no one system of acting such as natural or stylized. It is possible, also, that the boys—and indeed all the actors of the Elizabethan and Jacobean stage—were much rougher than we imagine them. They were the first actors to perform professionally for a large popular audience in England, and it would not be surprising if they had not yet developed much of the subtlety we associate with great acting in later centuries. What is certain is that Renaissance audiences were not looking for the psychological complexity that realism and naturalism have posited as a *sine qua non* of fine acting and that we expect almost as a matter of course. On the other hand, it is also likely those actors were capable of tapping energies from which our left-brained culture has completely separated us—some of the same energies that *kabuki,* not subjected to rationalism until after 1868, has always drawn on. The boy actors, sharing the same energies and profiting from close association with mature actors, may well have developed the technical skills in voice and diction, in movement and dance, that allowed them to impress audiences who were not looking for individualized characterizations but types.

What distinguishes the *onnagata* most clearly from the boy actor is the highly codified art passed on for generations in *kabuki* and constantly refined. Deriving from a reality that placed women in an inferior position, where they were expected to take up as little space as possible (figuratively if not literally), the *onnagata* created a manner of moving that required spatial concentration: hands held inside the sleeve, elbows against the body, knees together, feet pigeon-toed. To suggest the softness and gentleness of woman's movement required a spine of steel and muscles of iron; a stern discipline that resulted in shoulders that could gently slope; and a neck, chest, chin, and head that could bend, circle, and scoop ever so gracefully. By the mid–eighteenth century a rich vocabulary of movement and specific gestures had been created so that the actor could walk into a new role and create his character and blocking by finding parallels with older classics. Types were created, areas of specialization evolved. Somewhat like the actors of the *commedia dell'arte*, the *kabuki* actors could follow their "lines of business" and incorporate the equivalent of *lazzi*, both serious and comic, in building a new role.

Even though Robertson Davies suggests a complex training for the apprentice actors that compares in many ways with that of *kabuki*, the boy actors in no way appear to have created so fixed a code as we find in *kabuki*. Like young *kabuki* children, they studied voice, speech, and dance; learned the jig; studied gestures that were appropriate for certain situations; learned to wear and manipulate the heavy costumes; and practiced weaponry and fencing (Davies 1939, 31). But there is no detailed description anywhere of their style of movement, and Portia's allusion to the "mincing steps" she must turn into a "manly stride" in order to play her role as male is a shaky basis for comparison to Japanese maidens, even though westerners seem to favor "mincing" as an adjective to describe the latter.

I cannot stress too strongly that most of what we know about the Elizabethan and Jacobean actors and their performances is highly speculative. A number of recent studies have looked closely at the play texts and their approaches to women's roles played by boys or men, but because it seems unlikely that much else will surface to give us a firm basis for studying the actual performance techniques of the actors, I would like now to explore—again quite speculatively—the possibility of similarities or differences in the acting of female roles in England and Japan arising from the sexuality, and particularly the homosexuality, of the actors who played those roles. It is with some trepidation that I leap into the roiled waters of Renaissance sexuality and gender, since they are muddy enough already—perhaps necessarily so, given the "utterly confused" conditions that Foucault sees in the period (1978, 101). Many books and articles have contributed fascinating, thought-provoking— and often contradictory—insights into questions of impersonation, sodomy, sensuality, homoeroticism, and so forth. I do not propose to challenge these but simply to accept as a given the views expressed by such writers as Jonathan Goldberg in *Sodometries*, Alan Bray in *Homosexuality in Renaissance England*, and Bruce R. Smith in *Homosexual Desire in Shakespeare's England*. That is to say: during the Renaissance, there was no such category as homosexual, and, in Bruce Smith's words, "sexuality was not, as it is for us, the starting place for anyone's self-definition" (11). In short, one cannot distinguish between homosexuality and heterosexuality in the Renaissance except by bringing to bear an anachronistic concept of our own day in works that totally ignored such categories, works that conceived the world and express that world along very different lines.

This means that we, with our cubby-holes and concepts, heirs of a Cartesianism that had not yet arisen in Elizabeth's and James's days, must exercise great care when we look at the English boy actors, for we too readily associate female impersonation with homosexuality, drag queens, high camp, and such. The dangers that the moralists and Puritans, the antitheatricalists, saw in the boy actors was not *necessarily* the temptation to homosexual acts. Instead, according to Stephen Orgel, they feared that the boys' skill was so great that it would rouse the lust of men, turn them "effeminate," by which the Elizabethans meant "incapable of manly pursuits," too interested in love and clothing and other such vanities, including women (1989, 16). So unstable is our identity, the antitheatricalists believed, that we are constantly at risk, and both the boys who play at being women and the men who admire them as women may all too readily become what they are merely imitating. One comes away from the Renaissance world in England, France, and Italy (and there were, obviously, peculiarities in each country) with the impression that bisexuality ran rampant but was never recognized, categorized, or stigmatized as such.

Time and again the comments of the antitheatricalists (Prynne, Stubbes, Rainolds, and others) remind us how successfully the boys impersonated women. If we were to take their testimony at face value we could conclude that the boy actors were past masters at female impersonation. "Beware the beautiful boyes," warns Rainolds, "transformed into women by putting on their raiment, their feature, lookes and facions" (34). An Englishman traveling on the Continent reported in

1611, with some surprise, that Italian actresses could actually perform as well as the boy players (Bentley 1984, 114).

Such comments by viewers, and the radical insecurity of identity that underlay many of the moralists' criticisms, point toward a portrayal of women that was, at least in Renaissance eyes, realistic. If there was no certainty as to what precisely characterized women, and what men, would not the actors attempt to base their impersonations on actual women that they could see and hear, women they perhaps knew and lived with? Could we not assume that they impressed spectators with their skill by the degree of resemblance they were able to achieve? Would they have conceivably attempted to fabricate some androgynous creature, drawing both on the feminine qualities of a young boy and whatever nascent masculinity they might enjoy? Boys of thirteen or fourteen? It seems improbable.

Although records are certainly incomplete and the distance is great, by and large the picture of the boy players that emerges is one of young lads drawing on the natural childish or adolescent charms of their tender years to imitate as skillfully as they knew how women as they saw them or knew of them through report. Using their young imaginations and the help of older men who instructed them, they could no doubt achieve striking impersonations that ranged from the sweet young innocence of Juliet to the rambunctious assertiveness of Kate or the full-blown villainy of Regan and Goneril, playing in modes as realistic as the low-life characters of *Henry IV* and *Measure for Measure* or as heightened as the queens and ladies in *Hamlet* or *Cymbeline*.

When we turn to Japan we find a completely different picture: instead of repressing, or not even recognizing, homosexuality when it occurred, the Japanese had for centuries an established system of love between mature men and young boys that reminds us, in many details, of the *paiderastia* of Greece. It even had a name: *wakashudô*, shortened to *shudô*, the Way of Adolescents or, more blatantly, Boy Love.[1] As Paul Gordon Schalow points out in his masterful introduction to his translation of Saikaku's popular novel of 1687, *The Great Mirror of Male Love*, "Popular literature in premodern Japan did not depict male love as abnormal or perverse, but integrated it into the larger sphere of sexual love as a literary theme" (6). Indeed, it was often taken for granted that

---

[1]The phenomenon is studied, in English, in some detail by Watanabe and Iwata 1989 and in a solid introduction and notes by the translator, Paul Gordon Schalow, of Ihara Saikaku, *The Great Mirror of Male Love* (1990), 1–46. The latter volume includes an excellent bibliography, listing major Japanese items. Gary P. Leupp's *Male Colors* is the most recent and thorough study in a Western language of the phenomenon.

the young men playing *onnagata* roles were available for sexual favors, and *kabuki*'s history certainly contributed to such an attitude, for, from its beginnings, the performers had often been prostitutes. The great Yoshizawa Ayame began as one, and at least one writer suggests that "after Ayame nearly all *onnagata* lived this way throughout the rest of the Tokugawa period" (Laderriere 1984, 238). It is clear from the literature of the period and from scholarly studies of popular culture that *shudô* was an accepted part of *kabuki* life at least until well into the eighteenth century. Many, and perhaps even most, of the *onnagata* began as catamites and continued to practice this part of their "art" after they became actors. To what degree and until what age is, of course, difficult to determine.

What might be the results of such a system of Boy Love, and the experience of life as a catamite—or in more idealized terms as a young man receiving the protection and love of a deeply committed and caring mature male—and what would be the influence of all this upon the portrayal of women in *kabuki*? What I want to suggest is that, unlike the boys of Shakespeare's day who attempted to imitate the women they knew as carefully as they could, the young *onnagata* began by identifying *himself* with a womanly role, since in the Way of Boy Love it was understood that the boy would play the passive more feminine role while the *nenja*, or mature male lover, would be both literally and figuratively "on top." This would lead, it seems to me, to an androgynous self-concept because the boy *knows* he is physically a male, but he plays, both physically and psychologically, a role that has been identified in his culture with the woman. It also gives him an intimacy with the feminine, an identification with it that would be lacking in the English model, and this allows him to create his women's roles in what one might describe as a position straddling the sexes.

The androgyny of the young actor is suggested by a number of phenomena. In the early seventeenth century, for example, the face of the young adolescent boy, the *wakashû*, apparently became the ideal of feminine beauty, and this type of face (to which young women aspired) was known as the *wakashû-gao* or boy's face (Watanabe and Iwata 1989, 82). A contemporary parallel might be the admiration women feel (and have always felt) for reigning *onnagata*: today it is not unusual to find the face of the popular performer Bandô Tamasaburô used in women's cosmetic advertising.

I am suggesting that the women created by the *onnagata* are necessarily androgynous, creatures of artifice, in which the charm of the performance lies *not* in the exact imitation of woman but rather in the elaboration of something that appears to be quintessentially feminine but possesses at the same time the inner steel that we traditionally (and chauvinistically) think of as masculine. It is what Ayame describes as "the synthetic ideal," blending male and female characteristics, or what Gary Leupp in his masterful study of *Male Colors* calls "a titillating blend of female sentiment and male assertiveness" (177). The Japanese appear to have been particularly sensitive to this androgynous appeal. Within the *kabuki* (and actually in almost any form of Asian traditional theatre) handsome young male lovers are—to our Western eyes—perilously close to the feminine side of the gender continuum, with their delicate movements and high voices. Indeed, the role of the *wagoto* or "soft character," as this young lover is called, is usually the domain of the *onnagata*, and it is fascinating to see the same actor on one occasion play the courtesan lover, with her great inner strength, and on another play the feckless young male lover. The late Ganjirô II and his son, then known as Senjaku, were a famous pair of which Ganjirô played the man and Senjaku the woman. Now, since his father's death, Senjaku has assumed the name of Ganjirô III and with it his father's lover role, and his own son now plays the woman to his man.[2]

On the one hand we see Tokugawa Japan relishing sexual ambiguity, appreciating the sensuous appeal of the androgynous male or female both onstage and in the bedroom, and even building Boy Love into a system with rules of etiquette. Official condemnation there was, but it was a hardheaded, practical, reasoned condemnation from militarists and Confucian scholars. On the other hand we see the Elizabethan and Jacobean official condemnation of "sodomy," which, in all its vagueness, is associated with fearful and incomprehensible elements like heresy, witchcraft, and bestiality and is denounced with a hysterical emotionalism and irrationality that arises from religious conviction and fear of the unknown. The act that we today call *sodomy* was enjoyed and graphically portrayed in novels, letters, and hundreds of woodcuts in Japan of the seventeenth, eighteenth, and nineteenth centuries, but it was punishable by death in England. And yet, despite Puritan fulminations and literary or diaristic allusions, very few were actually executed for what they had apparently done because there was an unwillingness to recognize, or an inability to categorize, the action for what it was. A

---

[2]Another example of contemporary androgyny would be the male role players of so-called "Women's Opera," the *Takarazuka*, who display even more crossover characteristics than the *onnagata*, for they are never totally convincing as men, but they *are* the idols of thousands of adolescent girls who adore them, fall in love with them, and worship them much as the *wakashū* actors seem to have been worshipped in the seventeenth century. Leupp deals in great detail with androgyny and gender ambiguity in *kabuki*.

dramatic example of the confusion in the English mind at the time comes from the very peak of the social scale: King James I, who was both deeply religious and homosexual (before the concept had any meaning), could write in his defense of absolute monarchy, the *Basilicon Doron,* that one of the horrible crimes a king could never forgive was sodomy; yet he could then turn to write a letter to his beloved Villiers, Duke of Buckingham, whom he addressed as "my sweet child and wife" (Spencer 1995, 164).

But if conditions in England militated against an androgynous portrayal of women on the stage, there is one paradigm of the feminine that may have led English actors in that direction. If I am right in my supposition that the boy actors studied women more or less from the outside, they would have had several avenues of approach. The women they actually came in contact with would serve by and large as models for low, or perhaps middle-class, roles. Hearsay, or simply the accepted rules of class and male/female deportment, would give them general clues of behavior for many roles. And for the most exalted roles, they might consult courtly romances or poetry. But they also had a sublime paradigm, at least until 1603, in the queen herself. It is tempting to speculate on the portrait offered by Queen Elizabeth. If there is any historical accuracy in the huffing characterization created by Bette Davis and memorialized on occasion by Beverly Sills in *Roberto Devereux,* Elizabeth was a far cry from the quintessentially feminine, gently helpless, being so often impersonated by the *onnagata.* Indeed, she reminds us rather, in *kabuki* terms, of those evil women like Iwafuji, who are often played by *tachiyaku* and who present a consciously androgynous character. This should not be surprising when we recall that Elizabeth signed herself "Rex," rather than "Regina," and felt the need to assert herself in a "masculine" manner in a world where women were mistrusted and disparaged. Carole Levin, in her fascinating study of that monarch, *"The Heart and Stomach of a King,"* makes it clear that for herself and for many of her subjects Elizabeth was both king and queen. She even jokingly suggests to Phillip II of Spain that she might be husband to a Spanish princess (133)!

If Elizabeth was indeed a model for certain characterizations of women, what she offered was an androgynous model, blending power and vulnerability and presenting a façade curiously similar to that of the *onnagata:* face covered with the customary white makeup that gave an idealized complexion and helped to cover the pockmarks left by the inevitable disease; eyebrows painted; bewigged and costumed in forms and colors appropriate to sex and status. Moving perhaps in that nervous swagger favored by Davis, Elizabeth presents a fantastic royal icon, and it is tempting to imagine that it was staged occasionally. But how often could the Renaissance actor play a character of such regal position and formidable bearing? Perhaps in some few powerful and courageous women, and in the somewhat more frequent cross-dressed heroines that recur throughout the plays. But by and large, the boy actors probably turned more often to the less lofty models of women than they did to their monarch. They tended, in short, as I suggested earlier, more often to Nature whereas the *onnagata* tended more often to Artifice.

Artifice on the one hand and Nature on the other: we have arrived at the two poles of Renaissance English acting that have been debated endlessly for the past hundred years. Such a polarization represents an oversimplification of the phenomenon of acting and of the actor-spectator relationship. In the hands of a great actor, the high stylization and artifice implied by *kabuki* are *always* balanced by a recognition of the reality from which the stylization derives and by an inner conviction, strength, and identity that in Japan is known as "stomach art," *hara gei*. The *kabuki* spectator, like the opera lover, is perfectly able to admire the art of the actor, whether it is made up of high C's or moving eyebrows and crossed eyes, at the same time that he/she is moved to tears by the plight of the character. And so is the spectator of Shakespeare, as Gary Schmidgall makes clear in his brilliant chapter on "Technique and the Gemini Factor" in *Shakespeare and Opera* (1990, 188–203). Rather than a compromise between the warmth of Method acting and the alienation of so-called Technical acting, Schmidgall sees a "volatile, *yin-and-yang* coexistence of both styles" (203). And necessarily so in a theatre that "runs the full gamut between realistic dialogue that could have been heard in the street outside the Globe . . . and the gaudiest blank-verse bravura speech" (198).

And so I return at the end to the question of my title: boys, women, or phantasmal androgynes? Everything we know about Renaissance boy players in England—which is very little—and everything we know of European female impersonation in the Restoration theatre and beyond points in the direction of boys or young men impersonating women with enough success to cause Puritans to denounce their womanly wiles and Cavaliers to applaud their feminine charms. The impulse we see toward Nature and realism in English theatre, English gardens, and English architecture (when France, for example, was already falling under the formalist influence of classicism) would support the supposition that the boys were attempting an impersonation of women as they existed in reality without the rearrangement of their vocal and movement characteristics into stylized patterns. One might believe that a country that trimmed its gardens into symmetrical geometric shapes, following the ideals of a Le Nôtre, might produce that kind of stage woman, but a country where gardens, houses, and play structures had the asymmetry of unpruned Nature would probably produce actors who sought to create women as natural as the gardens they walked in. The shortness of the boys' careers suggests that, rather than creating a dream vision of women, they drew on their own preadolescent characteristics—all of which Hamlet mentions, by the way (2.2): unbroken voice, short stature, and beardless face. English sexual attitudes lead us to similar conclusions, for no matter how much the boy actors may have practiced buggery, there is scarce mention of it aside from the outraged Puritans and a few satiric allusions; and there was apparently never a belief that it was a way of life, or even a sexual orientation, since such categories simply did not exist. The boys must, then, have approached their women's roles not as women, from the inside, but as boys who studied women about them in order to learn how to behave, move, and speak.

The Japanese *onnagata,* on the other hand, walked in a garden that appeared to follow natural asymmetry but was rigorously disciplined, cut, pruned, and swept to the desired shape and texture. His practice of buggery was frankly acknowledged, and his career as a woman onstage (and frequently if not always offstage as well) lasted a lifetime. Having experienced the woman's role, as it were, from the inside, he had the freedom to create his own vision of the stage woman, ranging from the most vulgarly naturalistic to the most elegantly stylized. Following the tenets of Ayame, he created a synthesized portrait—part male, part female. Following the convictions of Chikamatsu, he fabricated a woman in that "slender margin between the real and the unreal" (Keene 1963, 389), where art lies. When we look at the *kabuki onnagata,* we see a phantasmal androgyne, and this is one reason that women in *kabuki* roles are generally considered unsatisfactory: they lack, it seems, the grotesque element that the male part brings to the portrait. Like the garden where he walks, the *onnagata* must be natural but not too natural; he must reflect the asymmetry not of Nature but of Art.

Works Cited

Bartholomeusz, Dennis. 1969. *Macbeth and the Players.* London: Cambridge University Press.

Bentley, Gerald Eades. 1984. *The Profession of Player in Shakespeare's Time.* Princeton: Princeton University Press.

Bray, Alan. 1982. *Homosexuality in Renaissance England.* London: Gay Men's Press.

Davies, W. Robertson. 1939. *Shakespeare's Boy Actors.* London: J. M. Dent and Sons.

Dunn, Charles J., and Torigoe Bunzô. 1969. *The Actors' Analects.* Tokyo: Tokyo University Press.

Ferris, Lesly, ed. 1993. *Crossing the Stage*. London: Routledge.

Foucault, Michel. 1978. *The History of Sexuality*. Vol. 1, *An Introduction*. Translated by Robert Hurley. New York: Pantheon Books.

Fujita, Minoru, and Leonard Pronko, eds. 1996. *Shakespeare East and West*. Richmond, Surrey: Japan Library.

Goldberg, Jonathan. 1992. *Sodometries: Renaissance Texts, Modern Sexualities*. Stanford: Stanford University Press.

Gurr, Andrew. 1992. *The Shakespearean Stage, 1584–1642*. Cambridge: Cambridge University Press.

Hyland, Peter. 1987. " 'A Kind of Woman': The Elizabethan Boy-Actor and the *Kabuki Onnagata*." *Theatre Research International* 12, no. 1:1–5.

Keene, Donald, ed. 1956. *Anthology of Japanese Literature*. Vol. 2. Rutland, Vt. and Tokyo: Charles E. Tuttle Co.

Kennedy, Dennis, ed. 1993. *Foreign Shakespeare*. Cambridge: Cambridge University Press.

King, Thomas J. 1992. *Casting Shakespeare's Plays: London Actors and Their Roles, 1590–1642*. Cambridge: Cambridge University Press.

Laderriere, Mette. 1984. "Yoshizawa Ayame (1673–1729) and the Art of Female Impersonation in Genroku Japan." In *Europe Interprets Japan*, ed. Gordon Daniels. Tenterden, Kent: Paul Norbury Publications.

Leupp, Gary P. 1995. *Male Colors: The Construction of Homosexuality in Tokugawa Japan*. Berkeley: University of California Press.

Levin, Carole. 1994. *"The Heart and Stomach of a King"*. Philadelphia: University of Pennsylvania Press.

Orgel, Stephen. 1989. "Nobody's Perfect: Or Why Did the English Stage Take Boys for Women?" In *Displacing Homophobia: Gay Male Perspectives in Literature and Culture*, ed. Ronald M. Butters, John M. Clum, and Michael Moon. Durham: Duke University Press.

Pepys, Samuel. 1970. *The Diaries of Samuel Pepys*. Ed. R. C. Lathan and W. Matthews. London: G. Bell and Sons, Ltd.

Pronko, Leonard C. 1967. *Theatre East and West*. Berkeley: University of California Press.

——. 1994. "Theatre East and West: Return to the Feast." *Contemporary Theatre Review* 1, no. 2:13–22.

Rainolds. 1599. *Th'Overthrow of Stage Playes*. London: n.p.

Schalow, Paul Gordon. 1990. *The Great Mirror of Male Love* (of Ihara Saikaku). Stanford: Stanford University Press.

Schmidgall, Gary. 1990. *Shakespeare and Opera*. New York: Oxford University Press.

——. 1994. *The Stranger Wilde*. New York: Dutton.

Smith, Bruce. 1991. *Homosexual Desire in Shakespeare's England*. Chicago: University of Chicago Press.

Spencer, Colin. 1995. *Homosexuality in History*. New York: Harcourt, Brace and Company.

Watanabe, Tsuneo, and Iwata Junichi. 1989. *The Love of the Samurai: A Thousand Years of Japanese Homosexuality*. London: Gay Men's Press.

Fusing *Kabuki* with Flamenco

The Creation of *Blood Wine, Blood Wedding*

Carol Fisher Sorgenfrei

*B*LOOD WINE, BLOOD WEDDING is a *kabuki*-flamenco fusion inspired by Federico Garcia Lorca's 1933 *Blood Wedding*, by Chikamatsu Monzaemon's 1703 *Love Suicides at Sonezaki*, and by the lives of these two authors. Its first performance was at San Francisco's Cowell Theatre, 8–16 March 1997, with previews on 6 and 7 March. Cast and musicians included performers from the United States, Spain, and Japan. Evolving over a two-year period, it was initially conceived by Yuriko Doi, artistic director of the Theatre of Yugen, as a vehicle for *kabuki onnagata*, Nakamura Kyozo. Yuriko had first worked with Nakamura for the 1994 American tour of *Sarome Kyu-Kyu No Dan*, a loose adaptation of Oscar Wilde's *Salome* originally created in Japan by Masakatsu Gunji for Tokyo's Tiny Alice Theatre. The play had not translated well into an American performance idiom, but Nakamura was keen to try another creative collaboration and he suggested *Blood Wedding*. In 1995 Yuriko commissioned me to adapt Lorca's play into dance-theatre work, fusing *kabuki* and flamenco.

The Bride would be performed by Nakamura in *onnagata* style; Leonardo, the lover with whom she elopes on her wedding day, would be performed by La Tania, a fiery female flamenco dancer based in northern California. All four of us could visualize at once the movement possibilities based on these dance vocabularies: the curving, flowing rhythms of the agonized but statuesque *kabuki* female encircled and entrapped by the high-shouldered, foot-pounding energy of the flamenco male. We all liked the idea of "gender-equity" that the casting implied. Beyond that, we were in the dark. Although we were all willing to experiment, no one had the slightest idea how the music would sound or how the dancers would create mutual interactions in terms of duets or new styles. We didn't even know what kind of costuming we would consider. But we leaped in and started gathering artists and applying for grants.

Yuriko and I have always been intrigued by cultural correspondences between Japan and Spain. Traditional art in both cultures emphasizes the conflict of desire and duty. The cultures share an obsession with honor, family, blood, purity, and death. Both feature complex, rhythmic, foot-pounding, sensual dance. Because Kyozo did not feel comfortable acting in English, and because La Tania is a dancer untrained in speaking for the stage, we planned to use a *joruri*-style narrator as is found in *kabuki* or *bunraku*. Thus the structure would be Japanese, the story Spanish. I decided to embark on a new translation before attempting the adaptation. This led to an immersion in Lorca's Spanish poetry that left me totally depressed. How could I come close to the beauty of the original, and how could I cut this magnificent poetry to create a work focused on dance? I was released from my gloom by a *deus ex machina* called the Rockefeller Foundation, from whom Yuriko hoped to obtain a grant. They were quite intrigued by our project, but the grants they offered were for new play development, not for translation or adaptation. So I metamorphosed from an unhappy adapter to an excited but somewhat confused playwright. In the end we didn't get the grant, but I did write an original play.

The first issue I faced as a playwright was finding a rationale for the *kabuki*-flamenco fusion. Dance adaptation doesn't really need a logical rationale; aesthetic choices require patterned unity or an intentional clash of styles that can be analyzed in terms of visual, musical, or movement vocabulary. Often, the "rightness" of dance aesthetics is visceral rather than intellectual. Plays, on the other hand, are more dependent on ideas and words. Even surreal, abstract imagery in scripted drama demands a logic of its own. I felt the play needed a specific locale in which its story might have occurred.

What historical and geographical options permitted a love story between the children of a Spanish and a Japanese family? The history of Spanish colonization in the New World offered an answer. For the first version, I set the play in central California in 1936. The Iberian colonizers, granted extensive land rights by the Spanish court, had retained a strong sense of class consciousness and racial purity, making distinctions between direct descendants of "peninsular" Spain and other groups such as Mexicans, mestizos, Native Americans ("indios"), and so on. Japanese migrated to California and elsewhere in the West in search of new lives or wealth during the Meiji and Taisho periods (especially from 1884 to 1924, when Japanese were legally excluded from further immigration to America). California's great central valleys provided farmland and jobs.

The main problem with this "realistic" choice is the politically and culturally sensitive issue of California's Mexican heritage. During the early twentieth century anti-Mexican sentiments among revisionist Caucasian Californians erased the actual Mexican historical contribution and created a fantasy heritage derived directly from Spain. Tourist events such as Santa Barbara's bogus "Old Spanish Days Fiesta" and invented foods such as "Spanish rice" were the result. Today California's Chicano (Mexican American) population is acutely aware of these facts, strenuously objecting to the depiction of the "fantasy of 'Spanish' California." I did not want to contribute to this racist history and therefore suggested a Mexican family. However, La Tania protested this choice because dancing the flamenco would be culturally inappropriate. I was caught in a dilemma: historical accuracy versus aesthetic accuracy. As a compromise, for the original San Francisco production I created a California family that felt itself to be the last bastion of Spanish "racial purity." However, I am now considering eliminating all references to California and setting the play in an unspecified world somewhere in a land once colonized by Spain—a conventional New World in some mythical dimension that the audience will simply have to accept, like Prospero's island. I hope to prevent the possibility of cultural/historical misunderstandings. The audience will be able to focus on the actor/dancers and their stories rather than on the question of whether the play is historically accurate.

The other "realistic" choice was to set the play in 1936, when an old Spanish-descended family might still maintain a distorted sense of ethnic superiority. It is also nearly the last moment until after World War II when a Japanese family could still legally own land, albeit only through the American-born daughter. Nineteen thirty-six was the year in which the pivotal Spanish civil war began the inexorable rush to World War II. It was the height of the depression, an era of social, economic, and political ambiguities. Finally, 1936 was the year Lorca was assassinated by the Spanish Fascists.

The Bride became the daughter of a wealthy Japanese strawberry farmer and the Bridegroom the son of an old, aristocratic Spanish landowner. Leonardo, the fiery lover with whom the Bride elopes, became a Spanish gypsy, as despised in the New World as in the Old. As in Lorca's original, the parents were primarily interested in a match of two wealthy families; part of Leonardo's forbidden nature was his poverty. I felt that during the depression, the need for economic security might be powerful enough for the old, traditional parents to overcome (or at least suppress) their inherent racial prejudices.

About a year before rehearsals were to begin, Yuriko took a research trip to Granada, Spain, to immerse herself in flamenco dance and Lorca lore. At the same time, I was struggling with several script problems. While researching Lorca I had fallen deeply in love with his poetry and was mesmerized by his life and death. I was also working on making the character of Leonardo more heroic, more charismatic. When Yuriko returned from Spain, we found that we were both Lorca-infected. His spirit simply would not leave us alone. Yuriko wanted Leonardo to quote Lorca's poetry, but I had trouble rationalizing that a poor gypsy would be able to do so. I wanted Leonardo to be more political, conscious of social injustice, a union organizer for oppressed farm-workers, ready to run off to Spain and join the Lincoln Brigade—in other words, a Lorca surrogate. Finally, with great fear and hesitation, I told Yuriko that Lorca would not let me alone, that he was sitting on my shoulder demanding to be let into the play. I took a deep breath and told her that he wanted to be a character in his own play; he wanted to narrate it. Amazingly, she loved the idea.

Yuriko and I have both worked in Japanese-Western fusion for decades, so we had no difficulty discovering performance and structural references to *kabuki*. Examples are the Bride's dance with her maids in which she is entwined in long orange-blossom streamers, a dreamy solo on the balcony in which she dances with a fan, the two *michiyuki* sequences (dance journeys to death), and the Bride's solo with the green silk obi-like scarf. One moment was especially delicious for us, as we utilized a typical *kabuki* evocation of eroticism while reversing genders: the Bride sensuously unwinds Leonardo's obi-like cummerbund. We also enjoyed dressing La Tania in male flamenco garb, evoking the male impersonators of the all-female *Takarazuka* who adore Western costume. We both easily visualized scenic devices and theatrical effects typical of *kabuki,* such as the sudden dropping of the silk curtain to reveal the set and the tossing of silken "spider threads" at the wedding. I also incorporated stylistic aspects of *joruri* chant into the narration.

Knowing less about flamenco I began to attend performances by La Tania and other flamenco dancers. I envisioned dances of pounding feet, swirling capes, and mimed galloping horses. The rationale for using flamenco was obvious, but why *kabuki?* Lorca is inextricably bound up in the flamenco universe. He wrote, preserved, and recorded songs for the genre and inspired theatrical works by stellar flamenco dancers. In addition, there were historical precedents for Japanese-Spanish dance fusions. At least as early as 1920, Michio Ito (the Japanese dancer who inspired and choreographed Yeats's 1916 *At the Hawk's Well*) performed Spanish-style dance. It is also notable that in 1929 the legendary Spanish dancer La Argentina (not to be confused with la Argentinita) performed at the Imperial Theatre in Tokyo. Her performance remains a direct inspiration for *butô* founder Kazuo Ono.

Despite all our research, the only Japanese parts were technique, whereas the story was all Spanish. With the addition of flamenco dance we were creating a recipe for a work that was two parts Spain but only one part Japan. We felt that we were privileging Spain and neglecting Japan. Lorca's original play highlights the Bridegroom's Mother, a vengeful widow who loses all and ends up alone. But our version needed to focus more on the doomed lovers. Both leading roles needed expanding, yet neither of them could have extensive dialogue. The intersection of these two problems—the need to enhance the Japanese aspect of the story and the need to increase the size of the leading dance roles—led to the incorporation of Chikamatsu's classic tale through the creation of the character of the Ghost of the Bride's Mother.

Kabuki actors are noted for their versatility, and they often play multiple characters. Consequently, we decided to expand Kyozo's role by creating two parts for him to play. In Lorca's *Blood Wedding*, the Bride's long-dead mother does not appear, but it is rumored that she did not love her husband—and there are hints that the Bride might repeat her mother's tale. I decided to embody the Bride's mother as a tragic ghost whose own loveless marriage foreshadows the Bride's fate. The Ghost of the Bride's Mother would be danced and spoken in Japanese by Kyozo, narrated and translated by a second *joruri*—an additional performer. Her story would be that of a Japanese picture bride.

The Japanese-American practice of obtaining picture brides became widespread between 1910 and 1920. The cost of returning to Japan to seek a wife became prohibitive for most immigrants, and those who remained in Japan for more than a month faced induction into the military. Consequently, marriages were arranged and ceremonies performed with the groom *in absentia*. The husband was known only from a photograph and letter—often doctored or outright falsified. Although most picture brides lived out their misery in silent resignation, some women were so abused that they committed suicide or ran away, abandoning husbands and children. Most of these *kakeochi* abandonments involved a lover. If found, the runaway lovers were shunned by the community, and the women were sent back to their abusive spouses.

Chikamatsu Monzaemon's 1703 *Love Suicides at Sonezaki,* written originally for *bunraku* puppets, portrays a young man hopelessly in love with a prostitute. Like Lorca's play it was based on an actual incident. The young man defies social and filial obligations by rejecting an arranged marriage and attempting to buy off his lover's contract to the brothel. However, a friend cheats him out of his money. The distraught lovers, faced with economic ruin, social castigation, intolerable conjugal prospects, and a lifetime apart, sneak away and commit double suicide in the forest of Sonezaki. The play is a clear analogue for *Blood Wedding*, sharing themes of star-crossed lovers, the pressures of a harsh society, family obligations, shame, and the conflict of love with honor.

I decided to base the story of the Ghost of the Bride's Mother on *Love Suicides at Sonezaki*. When we asked Kyozo to consider playing the Ghost in *bunraku* style, he was at first hesitant because *ningyo-buri* (puppet-style *kabuki* movement) is exceptionally challenging. His ultimate performance was so striking that some members of the audience literally believed the Ghost was enacted by a wooden puppet rather than a live actor. We felt that one justification for using puppet-style performance for the Ghost was the pervasive presence of unseen forces manipulating the fates of the characters in all the stories. The black-robed puppeteers seem to Westerners (and to modern Japanese as well) to represent the uncaring yet controlling powers of darkness, fate, society, heredity, and so on. Shuji Terayama used puppeteers this way in *Jashumon* (1971), as did Masahiro Shinoda in his 1969 film version of Chikamatsu's *Shinju Ten no Amijima* (translated as *Double Suicide*).

Because Lorca was narrating a tale based on *Blood Wedding*, it became essential that the Japanese narrator be Chikamatsu, the author of *Love Suicides at Sonezaki*. The narrators now became characters based on historical figures with their own needs, desires, and fears. What had been a simple framing device with purely functional narrators had now become a third or outer story, a kind of reflection on the inner dance-dramas. The lines between the inner and outer plays began to blur. For example, at one point Lorca begs Leonardo to go to Spain and save him from death at the hands of the Fascists. Continuing this blurring effect, Yuriko had both narrators enter the play as wedding guests.

Using Lorca and Chikamatsu as characters created several lively disputes with Yuriko. She never wavered from calling the framing device of the two playwrights "a brilliant idea," but she was concerned that the play's emphasis would shift from dance to language and ideas. Yuriko's strengths as a director are in visual imagery and movement rather than in dialogue or psychological nuance, and Theatre of Yugen has a following that expects a certain type of production. In addition, our two star dancer-actors would not be pleased to have second billing to a couple of dead playwrights. As a writer I became quite taken with having the two playwrights debate aesthetic and cultural theory and with their having a relationship and a plot of their own. The characters were developing real lives and demanding to be heard. One of the hardest things for me was cutting so much of their dialogue.

At some point in the early summer of 1996, Yuriko decided to apply for another grant that required further changes. Would I write some songs, since the grant was for music theatre? I said I'd try. Yuriko began to present it as almost an opera; the script was becoming a libretto. Dorothy Moskowitz Falarski was recruited to write original music and to be music director for the live performance of guitar, *shamisen*, and *shakuhachi*. Although Dorothy had composed and performed for musical theatre, jazz, and children's theatre and had studied ethnomusicology at UCLA, most people remembered her from the sixties. Dorothy had been a rock star, singing, recording, and touring with bands such as "Country Joe McDonald" and "The United States of America." "I used to get stoned and go to Dorothy's concerts," our techies would say in awe. Dorothy's contribution was decisive and wonderful, but we didn't get the music-theatre grant either.

Our first reading of the play occurred 23 September 1996 at Nô Space, the Theatre of Yugen's small theatre in San Francisco. Some of the actors were members of the Theatre of Yugen company; others were invited because someone thought they might be appropriate for the show. Both Lorca (Lluis Valls) and Chikamatsu (Mikio Harata) were so good that there was little doubt that the roles would go to them.

That version of the play was sixty pages long, and I had promised Yuriko that the final script would come in at forty pages to leave plenty of time for dance and music. The comments that night suggested several significant changes that needed addressing. The two most important were liberating. First, in order to make Leonardo more likable for a contemporary American audience, it was suggested that we cut the wife and child that Lorca gave him. This not only solved character and script problems, but it eliminated an actor—a big budgetary consideration. And it permitted me to expand Leonardo's role as a charismatic leader of oppressed *campesinos*. Second, everyone strongly felt that as Lorca and Chikamatsu spoke the lines or translated for the doomed lovers, they were also speaking for themselves. Why not make them lovers, tragically unable to cross the boundaries of time, space, and culture? This idea riveted me. It was perfect, and it helped underline the theme of forbidden love. The historical Lorca had been gay, trapped in an unforgiving macho world. As for Chikamatsu, his sexuality is unknown, but he lived in an age that did not discriminate against homosexuals. Indeed, same-sex love was rather common in Japan, with older men serving as mentors for their youthful male lovers.

As I cut and transformed the play prior to our November auditions, I was forced to confront the question of why these two ghostly playwrights, now sexually attracted to one another, needed to rewrite their respective masterpieces. A simple desire to collaborate was not enough. Eventually I turned not only to their arguments about art and culture but to their lives. The unbearable tragedy of Lorca's murder at the age of thirty-eight struck me. He had been such a passionate character, so full of life, and he was ready to embark on what he saw as his first really mature work. Chikamatsu, on the other hand, lived over seventy years and by all accounts became greatly respected as a writer. Gradually, the outer story (that is, the playwrights' framing tale) became a *nô* play in which the tormented ghost of Lorca is finally eased by the ancient wisdom and wistful love of Chikamatsu's spirit. Like the *shite* in *nô,* Lorca must relive and rewrite his past over and over, until he can be free of attachment. This story became intertwined with the two inner tales.

Casting was an intriguing exercise. We sought actors skilled in either Japanese or Spanish dance. *Kabuki* is an art that combines dance and acting, so it is reasonable to assume that someone trained in *kabuki* has both skills. However, finding flamenco dancers who can also speak on stage is not exactly easy. Casting choices often meant finding a great actor who was an acceptable dancer, or vice versa. This situation affected the script. As an illustration I will use the story of Aldo Ruiz, whom we cast as the Bridegroom. La Tania felt confident he would be wonderful in the role—a key element of which was to be a final flamenco duet in which he and La Tania (the Bridegroom and Leonardo) fight to the death. A handsome, skilled, and charismatic flamenco dancer originally from Mexico, Aldo was sent more flowers than anyone else in the cast. Who wouldn't fall in love with him when he danced? But it was a different story when he opened his mouth. I felt a little like a character in *Singing in the Rain* as I cleverly rewrote scenes so that all Aldo had to say was, "Pero, Madre . . . " as the Mother interrupted with phrases like, "Quiet! Let me speak. . . . " And then Aldo would dance off in a whirl of stamping feet and lifted chest.

During two weeks of choreographic workshops in January that preceded formal rehearsals, Kyozo and La Tania learned from each other and taught the rudiments of their traditional dance styles to the cast and other members of the workshop. These workshops revealed to both La Tania and Kyozo that their dance vocabularies had much in common. Beginning with an appreciation of musical rhythms, they graduated to foot movements and the relationship of feet to the floor, to their respective spinal configurations, to hand and arm gestures, and to the incorporation in dance of costume and props. In the process they discovered connections. Not only would they each demonstrate the purity of their dance forms in the play, but they would be able to create new forms incorporating both styles. Kyozo especially became excited and completely rechoreographed a solo he had created for himself in Japan. This piece is the Bride's dance with the green scarf, which Kyozo decided to perform to flamenco guitar rather than to *shamisen.* Virtually the entire dance is *kabuki,* except for the hands. Kyozo discovered that certain female flamenco hand gestures that create a kind of figure-eight are almost exactly like certain female hand gestures in *kabuki.* The major difference is that in *kabuki* female characters would never spread apart the fingers, whereas in flamenco separated, sinuous fingers are highly significant. He daringly incorporated the flamenco hands into his *kabuki* dance, as the Bride dreams of the man she loves but can never have. To me this was the essence of fusion dance.

In terms of setting, Yuriko created a bare dance space encircled by two curving ramps and an upstage runway parallel to the proscenium. Behind that was a series of paper screens and scrims on which danced shadow puppets and the huge silhouettes of live actors. One of our earliest images for the play's opening was the shadow of the Mother cutting open the paper screens with a knife, creating a wound through which she enters. One set of screens opened to reveal the *bunraku* sequences. Behind the screens and scrims, two high platforms served as the Bride's balcony and the perch for the Moon. In act 2, when the elopement is discovered, streamers of China silk fell from above each time an actor said "Blood." Red lights made the streamers into waterfalls of blood; later, in the forest, green lighting transformed them into giant trees. After the fatal flamenco duel, the three *kurogo* pull down the streamers, leaving the stage bare. The Mother and the Bride slowly go up their separate ramps, as Chikamatsu and Lorca repeat the phrase "Alone, forever. Forever alone."

Part II: The Symposium. A Panel Discussion
on Crosscurrents in the Drama
East and West

[*Editor's note:* This is a condensed version of the panel discussion that took place among six distinguished artist-scholars of Asian theatre: James Brandon, Samuel Leiter, Leonard Pronko, Farley Richmond, Carol Sorgenfrei, and Andrew Tsubaki.]

BRANDON: This type of conference is wonderful because it causes things to come together in my head that otherwise might have continued to float around separately. In this brief time, let me make two points. One is from the perspective of a Western director who tries to find values within Asian materials and techniques that can be carried over into new theatre pieces created for American audiences. In Asian performance we find wonderful examples of how an audience perceives the theatrical performance on many levels simultaneously. First, the audience perceives the character and story—something that occurs in all theatrical events. Second, it perceives and responds to the actor, the musician, the dancer—that is to the living artists who are embodying the story and characters. Third, the "genre," the art form within which the artist and the story is enfolded. Fourth, the audience recognizes this is a theatrical event and not reality. Fifth, the audience is aware of its own existence in the time and space of the performance, and finally, the theatrical event exists within the larger social construct around it. When we recognize that audiences can have these multiple levels of perception at performances of *kabuki* or *kathakali* or *Wayang Kulit,* we are immediately aware of the limitation with Western realism. Realism is only concerned with the first level of audience response and ignores or specifically invalidates the others. Let me show a three-minute video clip to illustrate these levels, from *Kabuki Mikado,* a version of Gilbert and Sullivan's operetta that I directed at the University of Hawaii last fall. This is the version of "The List Song," as revised by four student dramaturgs and myself to fit the Hawaii audience of 1996.

[Note: The version of "The List Song" contains revisions that address the contemporary Hawaiian experience and uses such Asian devices as the *koken* to assist with props.]

In this song all of the levels that I have mentioned operate. And second, contrary to the received wisdom that stylization interferes with genuine emotional expression, we have marvelous examples in Asian performance that highly artificial, codified techniques of acting strongly support and indeed increase the emotional "truth" of acting. [This] reminds me of interviews I had with the chief puppeteer in the major *bunraku* troupe, the chief chanter, and the chief *shamisen* player. I asked them how they trained, how they learned as children. As we all know, the standard system in Japan is to copy your master. [But] those artists said, "We do not copy our masters. Of course we *watch* our master and we learn. But no two human beings are alike, so it is impossible for me to copy my master. I have to internalize my art, make it my own. Then I can become a great artist." This is a wonderful illustration of a solution to what might seem to be impossibly opposite goals: to "replicate" and to "create" anew.

LEITER: I'd like to begin by pointing out how, when you go to the theatre today, you're probably hardly aware of the degree to which . . . Eastern conventions have become an accepted, hardly noticeable, part of the Western theatrical experience. Things that one hundred years ago might not have been part of this experience are now ones we take for granted. This was brought home to me rather sharply recently when I went to a series of four or five plays in New York. . . . Every one of those American and English plays had something that very likely originated in Asian theatre. One play had a revolving stage, another had visible stagehands . . . moving scenery in front of the audience, another had a kind of suggestive scenic minimalism that was obviously unavailable a century ago. Of course, the question arises as to whether these "influences" came in directly from Asia or . . . stemmed from such things as William Poel's late-nineteenth-century Shakespearean revivals or from other contemporary investigations into old staging conventions. Even if directors like Poel were responsible for some of these ideas, they only made it easier for audiences to accept and adopt them when Asian theatre began to have an impact. . . . What was the nature of the reception of Asian theatre in the West, particularly in America, during this century? From how many directions was it arriving? Was it coming not only from the theatre but also from the print media? And in what form was such printed information becoming available? Today, because of Jim Brandon's pioneering work, we have *Asian Theatre Journal,* of which I'm very proud to have become the editor. But before *ATJ,* where did scholars publish . . . [on] Asian theatre? . . . How did the general public come in contact with Asian theatre in written material, other than in books? Well, there were a couple of popular theatre journals with a widespread readership. If you go back to the beginning of the century, probably the most popular one was *Theatre Magazine,* a very beautiful periodical that lasted from the turn of the century to 1931. . . . The most important periodical, and the one that . . . lasted the longest was *Theatre Arts,* which started in 1916 and went out of business in the early 1960s. [It] . . . served all the purposes of the more specialized journals we have today. It was written for an informed, educated audience including theatre professionals as well as the average theatre lover who had neither a professional [nor] academic interest. You could buy it at your major newsstands and by the early 1940s [it] was being sold to subscribers in forty-one countries. You could walk into a doctor's office in Singapore and see it on the table. So it was an international journal that had a tremendous impact. . . . There was a remarkable amount of Asian-related material covered, especially from the magazine's inception until World War II [when] suddenly there's a dropping off. . . . But when you look at the preceding period you see that all this concern we have today with multiculturalism in the theatre is really a case of reinventing the wheel. There is an intense fascination with Asian theatre, with India, Bali, Java. And while Japanese theatre is represented, it is by no means as central as some of the more unusual or esoteric—for most of us—forms of Asian theatre at that time. So there's this remarkable reception of Asian theatre, which also includes a series of Asian plays that were constantly being produced in American universities, little theatres, community theatres, and so forth, and that were obviously having an influence because they were being done so frequently. The most popular of such plays were the Indian play *The Little Clay Cart,* Klabund's version of the Chinese play *The Chalk Circle* (which would inspire one of Brecht's greatest works), *Lady Precious Stream,* and the American ersatz Chinese play *The Yellow Jacket,* which was accepted as a Chinese play because it closely emulated popular conceptions of Chinese opera. Then . . . the war came along, and the amount of reportage dropped off. . . . After the war, Asian-related articles were barely noticeable for several years. . . . In 1948 the management of *Theatre Arts* changed hands, and the magazine became a glossy one with a decided emphasis on the commercial theatre. . . . The more serious investigations of Asian theatre increasingly became the concern of the newly arisen academic theatre journals, although they too paid the East only sporadic attention at first. Fortunately, the postwar era saw the development of large-scale touring, with classical Chinese and Japanese companies, for example, making revolutionary trips to the West. . . . Anyway, I continue to find this subject of reception worth investigating because of the inevitable effect Asian theatre had on Western ideas of theatre.

PRONKO: I want to go back to a few things that people had said, and I'm probably going to misquote a lot of you. I remember Paul Lifton said something about Wilder's ignorance of Chinese theatre or of Asian theatre and suggested that it was perhaps that ignorance that allowed him to be more creative. I find that to be a very thought-provoking idea. Mark Ringer was talking about Mnouchkine's *kathakali* and how she had transformed . . . that, and I [had seen] her *kabuki* productions, particularly *Richard II*. When I met her, I asked her about it. "Would you call this *kabuki?*" I asked, and she answered, "I'd call it *kabuki imaginaire.*" And I thought, "Well, that's exactly right." And I began to wonder whether this imaginary *kabuki,* our own dream vision of these Asian forms, rather than an authentic, imitative version, might . . . allow us to create the most interesting theatre, a kind of theatre that speaks in the most lively way to our audiences. One reason I say this is because when I first began doing *kabuki,* in 1965, I had been to Japan for six months but I had never studied the techniques of performing *kabuki,* and so I thought, "Well, let's do these two plays (which I had never seen). . . . " And we did both of those plays in high *aragoto* style, and the audiences ate it up. Well, the more I learned about *kabuki* (it was after this that I started studying Japanese dance and got into the *kabuki* training program at the National Theatre) . . . , the closer I tried to get to the authentic Japanese *kabuki.* One day, one of my best friends, my oldest friend, said to me, "You know, Leonard, I think I liked the very first production you did best of all." And I thought to myself, "Well, maybe he's got a point. Maybe what we need is not to know too much." Then I reflected on Brecht and his understanding of the Peking Opera. It seems to me that Brecht's misunderstanding of Peking Opera was much more fruitful for the future than an understanding might have been. When Farley Richmond was talking about some of the Indian productions of Brecht that had specific agendas that sometimes betrayed Brecht, I thought, "That's exactly what Brecht deserves, because he did the same thing to Marlowe, Shakespeare, Schiller,

Gay, and others. He deserves it much more than Shakespeare, for example, does at the hands of wildly conceptual contemporary directors."
Then I began to think of what Evan Winet had said about Artaud's misunderstanding of the Balinese theatre. And I thought, "That misunderstanding of the Balinese theatre was much more fruitful than perhaps any understanding of it might have been." What has arisen from that misunderstanding is further misunderstandings of Artaud's misunderstanding, and those too have been very fruitful. . . . Perhaps they are fruitful precisely because they are doing what Artaud thought theatre should do, that is, dealing with these spaces, the openness of things . . . rather than in what he called dead ideas . . . because ideas, by the very fact that they are ideas, are dead. Artaud wanted us to deal with things that are constantly evolving, with living things, and that—on a certain level at least, the level of Artaud and Brecht if not of John Doe—is what misunderstanding allows us to do. It can be more dynamic. . . . In closing, I would like to say that I don't believe in cultural imperialism: I don't think it exists. Political imperialism in which I appropriate your property and you no longer have it, that definitely exists; but . . . no matter how I "appropriate" your art, you still have it. Imperialism means imposing our ideologies—political, spiritual, etc.—on the Other, on the target culture and denigrating that culture; it means appropriating their material wealth, their spices, their oil, or whatever. But when we appropriate spiritual or aesthetic ideas, that is the opposite of imperialism. And that is what most of us are interested in doing: not *appropriating* the Other, but *embracing* the Other. I don't call that imperialism; I call it brotherhood.

RICHMOND: Basically my ideas relate to the future as I see it developing [in] technology. . . . Many of us now have access to much more information about Asian theatre than was available only a few years ago. Rapid access to library information both here and around the world, rapid access to experts in other parts of the country and elsewhere in the world via e-mail, the World Wide Web, and the potential to provide textual information, as well as photos, videos, and sounds, allow for experts in widely separated locations to receive and send enormous amounts of data. That was simply not possible a few years ago. It struck me when Sam Leiter was talking about the *Asian Theatre Journal* that the *Journal* is a likely candidate to put on the WWW. It ought to be accessible not only to a small number of people but to many people around the world. [Moreover, there is the] potential for artists to interact through technology. The resources are beginning to be developed so that actors, directors, playwrights, designers may interact and share ideas among themselves in a live environment. For example, Carol Sorgenfrei [in her eloquent] presentation yesterday [spoke of traveling] between Los Angeles and San Francisco to consult with artists involved with [her] production. . . . It is entirely possible that she may have saved herself time and money by using technology to link with other artists with whom she was working. It is now possible to join in the discussions that shape a production through live interaction with artists in rehearsal halls hundreds of miles away. This led me to speculate that a *kutiyattam* drummer in India might [well] accompany *kutiyattam* actors in London through the technology that is becoming available, and audiences in two different parts of the world will be able to participate in the event that is being created live in these two very distant locations. And others around the world may beam in on their artistic presentations.

Think of Artaud's experience witnessing Balinese at the Paris exhibition. . . . It is quite possible in the near future that people like Artaud, living in different parts of the world, may explore the vast cultural resources of other societies through the WWW or through live simulations, just as Artaud explored the simulated world of Bali . . . brought to Paris. Fusion performances of all kinds may be envisioned that are similar to those which have been discussed at this conference, simply because of the new technological innovations.

Now you might well ask, "Is this not a new kind of cultural imperialism? Will such opportunities just be for those who have 'access,' especially those in the Western world, for those who are privileged to have equipment and connections to these electronic resources?" And I must say that of course that may be true, at least initially. But wasn't Broadway only available to those people in the late nineteenth century who had the resources to travel to the city to see the works that shaped our thinking about these periods? Broadway was only a dream to the vast majority of Americans until rapid transportation and the automobile became a reality.

Think of the profusion of videotapes, films, photographs about Asian theatre that were not available in the sixties when Jim Brandon was showing examples to his graduate students in Michigan. Many of us were seeing materials such as these for the first time. Most of us had no access to live performances of these materials in those days. Now it's possible to see vast quantities of such material, many of them live. . . . I would conclude that we are on the verge of an explosion of access to vast quantities of information, much more than was then dreamed of. Much more exciting things will occur as a result of technological innovation.

SORGENFREI: Like most of us I've spent considerable time brooding over issues such as cultural imperialism and appropriation. . . . As several of the papers and panelists have noted, creative borrowing often creates great art, but there are and can be abuses. I think the problem lies in the questions we ask. "What is the artist's responsibility to root cultures from which she derives ideas? When is the artist behaving as a tool (conscious or not) of imperialism? What damage is done to culture by theatrical intervention or borrowing?"

Now these are significant ethical issues deserving serious analysis, but my sense is that they may be the wrong questions. . . . They are loaded and leading questions. . . . They derive not from analysis of artistic goals, but from Western liberal guilt. . . . There is a kind of Marxist-Darwinian wallowing in self-hatred that such guilt implies, as though all members of an imperialistic culture are imperialists by nature. And there is a concomitant sense of moral superiority in the recognition of our evil, imperialistic tendencies which makes us self-flagellate and cry out "mea culpa"—even when there is no crime. This is not to imply that cultural imperialism is a myth. . . . Cultures can, of course, be damaged by the violent (or even the invited and desired) imposition of alien concepts. [It can happen with] the physical theft or destruction of material treasures, such as the British theft of the Elgin marbles or the Nazi burning of Jewish and "decadent" books and art. A culture can be damaged by the imposition of twisted ideas about that culture which are then incorporated and believed by the culture. The imperialist culture need not be foreign: look at the horrors inflicted on artists, scientists, intellectuals, traditional theatre, art, architecture, and Buddhist artifacts in China during the Cultural Revolution. But it is not clear that damage was inflicted by Gauguin's Tahitian paintings, or Artaud's psychotic musings on Balinese dance, or Yeats's imaginary *nô*, or even by Brook's *Mahabharata*. Would it have been better if Shakespeare had set *Othello* in Bankside, or had written *The Merchant of Stratford?*

The root cultures, peoples, or works in such cases are not damaged by cultural appropriation—the worst that can be attributed to such borrowing is the creation or perpetuation of negative stereotypes [that] can result in racism and even genocide, but that is not the fault of the artist or her work of art but of the misuse of the work by others—politicians, social engineers, and so on. The root culture remains intact, regardless of misinterpretations or slanders. All artists, by their nature, appropriate everything they experience. They appropriate it, they transform it into personal expression, and they return it to the world. Others are free to appropriate the new work, to be inspired by it, or to be offended by it.

So what are the right questions to ask? One, is the cultural appropriation done to create a new artwork of beauty and merit, or is it merely for the sake of exoticism? That seems to me to be a real travesty, for exoticism for its own sake is usually vulgar and seldom revelatory. Two, was the appropriated material freely given and available to all, or was it obtained through theft, trickery, or other nefarious means such as plagiarism? . . . Three, is the artist presenting the appropriated material as an anthropologically correct item, or are the changes, incorporations, recontextualizings, and so forth made explicit? I'm sure there are other tests we might put as well, but the key issue seems to be a healthy respect both for the root culture and for the new work. . . .

As a playwright I need to say that all scripts are by nature both the beneficiaries and the objects of cultural appropriation—and often of cultural imperialism as well. Every time a director, an actor, a designer, a critic, or a dramaturg uses or interprets my work, that work has been appropriated by another. What I created is transformed to something which others desire it to be. The culture of the appropriating (imperialistic?) entity colors the way my work is seen and heard; it colors the way it is presented, explained, or understood. Each member of the audience imposes his or her cultural concepts on my play. . . . Is this a problem I should be concerned with? No, in fact it is the essence of theatre, which is a collaborative, transformative, constantly shifting, ephemeral art. I think that the experience of the playwright is analogous to that of the "root culture" and that ultimately, all art is fusion art, all art is appropriation. The dangers lie not in borrowing, not even in misunderstanding, but in the potential for self-hatred and destruction of the root culture.

And finally, I want to talk about cultural imperialism from the point of view of theory. Currently, Western performance theories are being applied in what I see as a frightening, promiscuous fashion. Western theory which was developed to understand limited areas of the West is applied to artists from Korea to Papua New Guinea to Nigeria. To me, this imposition of Euro-American theories is a far more serious form of cultural imperialism than the other. . . . These true imperialists are those with specific social agendas which they attempt to impose upon others—agendas which may be noble and useful in the circumstances for which they were developed but which become grotesque distortions in other situations. In other words I am opposed to ethnocentric theorists who attempt to force their personal brand of global political correctness down the world's collective throat. Such theorists take potshots at easy targets by using sophisticated Western concepts such as feminism, Lacanian analysis, anthropological theory, and so forth. . . . The result is further misunderstanding in the high-minded guise of theory. As I suggested earlier, this type of imposition of theory onto cultures for which that theory is irrelevant results from Western liberal guilt and from overly zealous ideas of social engineering.

TSUBAKI: I decided to give a title to my presentation: "A Message to the Fourth Generation Asian Theatre Specialists." I want to emphasize to them the importance of training in any Asian theatre forms. Asian theatre forms are sustained by their distinct styles, and unless you learn them with your own body you can't really know what they are. Jim Brandon delineated what each form involves; as a result, its style is a vocabulary of Asian theatre. If you don't know that vocabulary, you can't really talk about it, or do it. I'm very impressed by a number of presentations in this symposium by younger scholars as well as, of course, older ones. In choosing my subject for the initial presentation in this round I decided to address especially the fourth generation specialists. . . . So the members of the first generation are Earl Ernst, Faubian Bowers, Donald Keane, Gargi in India, and P. G. O'Neill in England and so forth. Second generation is us: Brandon, Pronko, Richmond, Leiter, Benito Ortolani, myself, and Shozo Sato, people like that. Third generation is Carol Sorgenfrei, Elizabeth Wickman, Kathy Foley, Yukio Goto, a lot of University of Hawaii graduates and Pomona-related people, and somebody very unique and talented like Zavika Selper in Tel-Aviv University, who has a lot of actual training in three forms, *kabuki, nô, kyôgen*. And the fourth generation is the youthful group who are now teaching or are about to do so in higher education: Jonah Salz in Kyoto, Lawrence Kominz in Portland, David Furumoto from Hawaii, who may be coming back to teaching. We have a number of you folks out there.

When one specializes in Asian theatre, first of all, one needs to acquire a language to communicate with one's own master teachers and for your own research. One needs to do that sooner or later [in order to train] the actors in the production of replication or fusion theatre. Most of us did it after we finished the Ph.D. and after we started in permanent positions, except people like Shozo Sato who already had training in *kabuki* before he came to the United States, and maybe Kiyozo could be another example.

You need to learn and do authentic theatre before you do fusion theatre, if at all possible. In my case my initial training came in 1969, two years after I finished my dissertation on Zeami's *Yugen* at the University of Illinois. I went back to Japan for the first time in eleven years. . . . In four weeks of hot Tokyo summer, I studied three *kyôgens*, one *nô* play, and one *kabuki* play. I did it without any grant. I had my retirement fund from Ohio State and a little bit of savings, and the dollar was still strong in those days. My teachers were Nomura Mansaku in *kyôgen*, Nomura Shiro in *nô*, and Nakamura Matagoro in *kabuki*. They were all energetic and had time to teach me, and that was very important. It was summertime there and it was a slower time. But the situation is different today. Last summer I managed to see Mansaku and Shiro only once in my whole month's stay. Not that we didn't try, but I didn't have time and they didn't have time. It is more like they didn't have time. Taking any kind of consistent lessons from them is very, very difficult these days. I tried to help Richard Nichols to get some lessons from Mansaku and it was just impossible to arrange any lessons because he was so busy, so Richard ended up getting few lessons from his top disciple.

So, who are the ones teaching foreigners today? Interestingly, it's Don Kenny, Richard Emert, Beth Teel—those who decided to stay on in Japan and who have had considerable experience and exposure to Japanese traditional theatre. If you want to, I think you can find good teachers in Hawaii, Los Angeles, San Francisco, New York to get started. . . . You still have, I think, some ways to get to countries in the Far East. There are a lot of teaching jobs, particularly dealing with English, or you can find work as a computer specialist. Get there and do something; find time to go to the master teachers and explore your possibilities.

BRANDON: For the creative artist, "misunderstanding" is not the right word. Because the creative artist makes his own work for his own audience, he steals from wherever he wants to. So, by and large, I don't think that's an issue. On the other hand, in terms of scholarship, if somebody's writing about a culture, and speaking for that culture, as we all do when we write as scholars, then there is an obligation to understand to the best of your ability. Here I think the anthropological terms of "emic" and "etic" are useful. The terms that we bring in from the outside are "etic" terms. We look at *nô* and say, "Is it tragedy or not?" That's an "etic" attitude, or "outside." On the other hand, if you use "emic" concepts, you're saying, "The Japanese describe *nô* in terms of *yugen* (mysterious beauty) or in terms of *hana* ('flower,' freshness and novelty) and so on." I think at this stage of our understanding of Asia it is very, very valuable for scholars to try to look at the theatre in "emic" terms. When we do that we will largely avoid these gross problems of speaking for another culture in our own terms. On the issue of "authentic" versus "fusion" performances, my view is that we can take a dozen different approaches in mixing different cultures in theatre—all the way from total creation like Brecht being a little bit inspired by China but 98 percent Brecht to what I call "replications," attempts at replicating in English and with our performers an Asian theatre form. I appreciate Leonard Pronko's comment that perhaps the more perfectly you replicate, the less free you are to express your own creativity. But, again, if we understand why that is, then we can accept it. I've made choices in directing where I say, "Well, that's the way it's done." I know it might be more interesting if I change it, but I'm not going to change it.

LEITER: I'd like to pick up on one thing that Jim Brandon said: that many people have this idea of authenticity versus adaptation, or absorption into a new form or fusion or whatever. I don't personally think there is such a thing as authenticity. It's always going to be an approximation, no matter if you have the access to the materials that Jim has at the University of Hawaii, or if the costumes are authentic, the wigs are authentic, the makeup is authentic, and so on. There are just too many things that are not authentic. The language, for example, is the most obvious. And if, for example, you have, as Jim has in his past productions, often used a female voice to do the *gidayû* chanting, it may have a quality that suggests the Japanese, but it's still English, and still a female voice. So there's going to be some kind of fudging in any case. I'd also like to go back to something else that Jim said: the distinction that theatre people often make in responding to the classical, highly conventionalized Asian theatre. Too commonly they react to it as if it were merely a matter of forms, or of conventions, with no truthful inner life. . . . There's an article in the new issue of *Asian Theatre Journal* that discusses this from the Chinese point of view, pointing out that Chinese classical theatre has a concept that's quite similar to the notions of mimesis and *monomane*. In other words the actor's truth, the actor's belief, is always absolutely essential; these forms could never have become as highly developed . . . if they were purely formal expressions. . . . Let me give you a very little known anecdote from the mid–nineteenth century that illustrates some of what I've been saying. . . . The great star Ichikawa Danjûrô VII was performing the lead role of Matsuô in *Terakoya,* a play known in English as *The Village School.* Matsuô is in a very tough situation because he must demand the head of his own child without the other person knowing that Matsuô is the child's father. This other person, Genzô, has to go offstage . . . commanded to chop off the child's head, and he must reenter with the head in a wooden box. At one performance, the actor of Genzô went offstage and did his supposed decapitation business, but when he reappeared he did so without the head. He'd forgotten the prop, as actors everywhere

are wont to do now and then. He had to ad-lib through the moment
. . . and finally excused himself and ran off to retrieve the missing prop
so that Matsuô could enact his climactic scene of head inspection. After
the performance the actor went to the dressing room of his master,
Danjûrô VII, to offer his profuse apologies. "I'm so sorry. I apologize.
I did this terrible thing. I came out tonight without the head. I don't
know what came over me. How could I possibly have done that?" His
magnanimous master forgave him but put his finger on what the problem was. "What did you do when you went offstage? Did you wipe your
brow?" "Yes." "Did you have a sip of tea?" "Yes." "Were you thinking of your lines?" "Yes." "Well, you shouldn't have been doing those
things. When you went offstage, you should have been thinking about
what your action was as a character, which is to decapitate the child and
to arrange the head for the ensuing inspection. You had to do this even
though nobody out front could see you. If you were truly in the character, from the moment you went off and came back on, you would
never have forgotten the head, period, because you would have been
playing the role. You wouldn't have stopped to focus on anything else."
That, I think, is a perfect illustration, from the 1850s, of a tradition
that shows us the depth of realism and honesty that goes into this kind
of acting, regardless of the poses and the makeup and all the rest of
it. You have to be true, regardless of form.

SORGENFREI: That story reminds me of something that happened
one night during the performance of *Blood Wine, Blood Wedding*. One
night Kyozo forgot to bring the knife onstage for the final duel to the
death. This is the moment where the doomed lovers are trapped in the
forest, and the Bride pulls out her knife. She wants them to commit
double suicide, but the character of Death stops them because fate has
decreed that the Bridegroom and Leonardo will kill each other in a
duel, a thrilling *flamenco* duel with two knives. Well, this time Kyozo
forgot the knife. So there they were onstage, struggling, and the Bridegroom appeared with his knife drawn, ready to fight. La Tania, who
plays Leonardo, grabbed Kyozo's knife hand, and suddenly realized it
was empty. She was in a panic, thinking, "How am I going to fight a
duel to the death without a knife?" Well, all the actors immediately
understood the dilemma, and without missing a beat, Chikamatsu
pulled out his folded fan and tossed it—slid it, really—all the way across
the stage floor to La Tania, who scooped it up and proceeded to dance
with it. It was the most thrilling thing, this fan-turned-knife, totally
theatrical and totally right. They danced and dueled and stabbed each
other, one with a knife and one with a fan, and the entire audience

believed that was how it was supposed to be. It was just such a beautiful moment!

TSUBAKI: When I was younger I was very concerned about how little Yeats knew about *nô* theatre or how little Brecht knew about Chinese theatre, but today I'm in the frame of mind that what they did was okay. The reason I fuss about, whatever you call it, these true-to-the-original performances is that this approach will put us into a self-correcting mode of operation. If we leave what Brecht did about Chinese theatre as is, Yeats about *nô* theatre, or Artaud about Balinese theatre, we are acknowledging that they got us somewhere new. They provided us some excitement. . . .

Leonard aptly demonstrated [this] once at the Kennedy Center, where he took his production of *Gohiiki Kanjincho,* which was a hilarious comedy in a style, say, 80 percent *kabuki,* and 20 percent Pronko. The Pronko *kabuki* was followed by a very authentic *kabuki* trainees' performance, very properly done, but it was so dull. I was really flabbergasted at seeing that contrast. In the final analysis, you need to have a spirit of imagination and creativity to make a performance interesting. If you are bound by "how correctly am I doing this?" then you get so intimidated . . . it is not fun. But when you are relieved from that, and yet you have some kind of, as I said, vocabulary or technique which can be applied effectively, then such a product will sparkle.

PRONKO: When I studied at the National Theatre my favorite teacher, Bando Yaenosuke (the one who slapped you when you made a mistake— a wonderful pedagogical method because it makes you learn very quickly), always said, "It's not *kabuki* if you only learn it from the outside. If all you do is learn the *kata,* that's not *kabuki.* You've got to bring it from the inside." And that's a slow process. Where do these *kata*—and I use the word in the generic sense, that is, any formal idea that the actor uses that's become part of the tradition—where do they come from? Some actor, somewhere, made a decision to do something because it was right, because it was the truthful way to handle a piece of business. If you look at the history of these forms, you see that this actor chose to do a piece of business with his left hand, not because it was more beautiful, because psychologically it came from inner motivations that made the left hand more appropriate than the right. I'm using a rather simplistic example, of course, but that's basically what goes on. One actor's choice out of many, both by him and by others, became traditional.

SORGENFREI: Yes, all these ideas are making me think about the concept of borders. Borders are permeable, they are arbitrary divisions, whether we consider national borders or the borders between cultures, genders, even time. . . . For example, take a culture like Bali. It is an island, a defined mass of land surrounded by water. You might think that it's easy to define its borders, but it's not. Balinese culture has influenced and been influenced by neighboring and distant cultures. It is in a constant state of flux. The fixed boundaries are permeable—tourists or conquerors or missionaries come and bring new ideas; travelers or tradesmen or pirates take Balinese ideas, clothing, food, skills to other places. Change is inevitable. . . . By insisting on the impermeability of cultural borders, we are being arbitrary rather than organic. Living things have permeable borders. Air, food, and water are ingested and then excreted back into the environment in new forms. . . . And I believe that cultures are organisms, constantly changing. Insisting on borders just creates ossification. We don't want to freeze the past. . . . It's simply another way of Orientalizing, of imposing cultural imperialism.

RICHMOND: All of the people on this panel have produced Asian theatre productions. As far as I know, their intentions in teaching Western theatre students has been to introduce them to a process of doing theatre that is different from our own. It has not been to train them to be Asian theatre artists. This process is very different from the process of psychological realism which Leonard Pronko spoke of earlier which has pervaded the work of Western theatre artists of this century. Their efforts have been to indicate that there are alternative ways to think of performance. And hopefully when the students who are exposed to the processes of Asian theatre go out into the world they will carry with them a knowledge of this alternative way of considering theatre. These same students may [then] enrich their own work in the Western theatre.

BRANDON: I love it when theatre practice relates to theory. Hearing people today, it struck me that when an American goes to Asia today and apprentices himself or herself to a master, we have totally reversed the possibility of cultural imperialism. Now we are the students, they are the teachers. A white American going through the experience of being in the inferior position changes you internally and changes you psychologically. It helps you get a much greater, more honest understanding of relationships between countries, between cultures.

Thornton Wilder's Minimalist Plays

Mingling Eastern and Western Traditions

Paul Lifton

*W*HILE HE WAS WORKING on *Our Town,* Thornton Wilder described the play in a 1937 postcard to a friend as utilizing "the technique of Chinese drama" (Wilder papers), and the "Chinese" features of the piece did not escape the notice of reviewers of the original production. Several of them compared it to *The Yellow Jacket,* which had debuted in New York over twenty-five years earlier. Robert Benchley, reviewing the play in *The New Yorker* on 12 February 1938, compared the Stage Manager to the old Property Man in *The Yellow Jacket.* He disliked the playwright's use of pantomime, which he regarded as "suited more for charades and other guessing games than for stage plays," and he concluded, "That several of Mr. Wilder's scenes emerge refulgent from all this sign language and wigwagging is a great tribute to his powers as a dramatist. It is all very charming when the Chinese do it, but Mr. Wilder did not write a charming play and we are not Chinese" (26). Many other critics also identified the Stage Man-

---

Parts of this article appeared in my 1995 book, *"Vast Encyclopedia": The Theatre of Thornton Wilder.* This article constitutes a further development of points and observations put forth in the book.

ager as a variant of the Chinese property man (e.g., Burbank 1961, 89; Eastman 1938, 944; Eaton 1938, 21) and other features of the play, such as the use of pantomime, as "Chinese" or quasi-Chinese as well. Wilder's interest in pantomime was in fact apparently sparked by a performance by Mei Lanfang, which the playwright witnessed in New York in 1930 (Haberman 1967, 85).

In addition to *Our Town,* several of Wilder's shorter plays in the minimalist vein also reflect Mei's influence and exhibit parallels, too, with other Asian traditional theatres besides the Chinese. On the other hand, he appears to have been uninterested in or unaware of many non-minimalist aspects of Asian theatre. His borrowing was always highly selective. Certainly the lavish, symbolic, and highly theatrical costumes and makeup or masks, the extraordinary and specialized vocal techniques, the exaggerated or symbolic gestures, and the acrobatic or the unnaturally restrained movements of the *nô, kabuki,* and Chinese opera find no counterparts in his dramatic universe.

This circumstance was almost certainly due in large measure to ignorance. In fact, despite being the first major American playwright to borrow extensively from Asian theatre forms, Wilder was not particularly familiar with representative works or conventions of those theatres. His knowledge was mostly secondhand. He had lived in China as a boy but had not seen any traditional theatre there. Even Mei Lanfang's performance was a demonstration of Chinese techniques rather than a fullblown production. Similarly, according to a letter of his dated 25 July 1961, Wilder initially encountered the *nô* through a description in Paul Claudel's *The Black Bird in the Rising Sun,* but he notes that he had already written his major minimalist plays by the time he read Claudel's account (Wilder papers). There is a tantalizing reference to "the supernaturalism of Japanese drama" in an unpublished journal entry for 28 September 1922 (Wilder papers), but the playwright first saw an actual *nô* performance in the late 1960s. Perhaps it was his very lack of firsthand knowledge that allowed him to borrow freely and imaginatively from the Asian traditions and to integrate his borrowings comfortably into his own unique dramatic style.

Wilder also incorporated into his drama elements borrowed from such traditional Western theatres as the classical Greek, medieval, Elizabethan, and Spanish Golden Age. This places the Asian techniques in his plays in a global context that reduces their "alien" quality for the Western spectator. In fact, perhaps Wilder's real importance lies in his creation of an unparalleled point of intersection for Western and Eastern theatre. Many of the anti-illusionistic devices he employs have close counterparts not only in the Chinese or Japanese traditions but also in

European forms as well. The bare stage is as typical of the Elizabethan, Spanish Golden Age, and medieval theatres as of the *nô* and Beijing opera (and Sanskrit drama). Direct address, anachronism (which permeates *The Skin of Our Teeth*), and juggling with the theatrical illusion and the dichotomy and yet identity of actor and character may be met with not only in Elizabethan comedy and the Tudor interlude, but also in *kabuki* and Chinese opera. Wilder cited nearly all these earlier theatres as precedents for his dramaturgical "experiments." By incorporating elements from all of them—often into the same play—and by utilizing techniques and devices shared by many traditions, East and West, he graphically revealed the fundamental bonds uniting Eastern and Western theatre; moreover, his departures from the sources that inspired him help to clarify the special genius that each possesses, the differences that make each uniquely vital and valuable.

The use of pantomime in combination with a scenery-free stage is the most recognizably and expressly "Asian" aspect of Wilder's theatre. Suggestion of object and action through pantomime is a hallmark of numerous Asian theatre forms, from Chinese opera to the *nô*, although it is not as commonly or consistently used in the latter as it is in the former. The "Chinese" quality of *Our Town* is perhaps nowhere more evident than when a character enters or leaves the Gibbs or Webb houses—as George does in act 2, for instance—and the actor is obliged to open the door and cross the threshold in pantomime. The pantomimic establishment of the door and high threshold at the entrance to a house is one of the most frequently described pieces of business in the Chinese actor's repertoire (e.g., Chen 1951, 39; Pronko 1967, 55).

The similarity in this instance may not have been due to direct borrowing, but certainly the general inspiration of Mei Lanfang's 1930 performance is abundantly evident in several one-act precursors of *Our Town* that Wilder published together in 1931. Throughout "The Long Christmas Dinner," for instance, the characters serve and consume invisible comestibles with invisible utensils; in "The Happy Journey to Trenton and Camden," the hot dogs purchased and devoured by the Kirby family are suggested through pantomime, as are the steering wheel, pedals, and gear shift of the family Chevrolet, which is represented by four chairs resting on a stationary platform. In "Pullman Car Hiawatha," the third "experimental" one-act in the volume, the Pullman car itself, like the Kirbys' automobile, is represented by a simple arrangement of chairs suggesting the berths and compartments. The actors are thus obliged to mime opening and closing doors when the script calls for them to perform these actions. At other times they must press invisible call bells to summon the porter or handle imaginary items that fall from the invisible upper berths. Wilder even incorporated pantomime into one of his least "minimalist" plays, *The Skin of Our Teeth*, in the second act of which Mrs. Antrobus is required to hurl an invisible bottle containing a letter into the ocean, and on another occasion her husband and daughter are required to interact with invisible animals.

Wilder's technique of representing vehicular travel with the aid of pantomime (in such plays as "The Happy Journey," "Pullman Car Hiawatha," and the late play "Childhood") is close to Chinese and other Asian practices, although one minor point of divergence lies in the fact that in Wilder's plays the "vehicles" and their occupants ordinarily make no forward progress. In Beijing Opera an actor who is meant to be seen as riding in a chariot walks between two stage assistants bearing flags with wheels painted on them (Chen 1951, 28; Arlington 1930, 46). A somewhat closer approximation of Wilder's method may have been used in the performance of Sanskrit drama. The famous opening scene of *Shakuntala,* which depicts King Dushyanta's headlong chariot ride in pursuit of a wild deer, was originally performed entirely in pantomime (that is, without benefit of chariot), although here, too, the performers probably did not remain stationary throughout (Raghavan 1981, 31). Perhaps the closest parallel to Wilder's method in Asian theatre practice—or at least the best-known one in the West—is the celebrated pantomimic depiction in Chinese theatre of a river crossing or other aquatic journey by nonexistent boat. Bertolt Brecht (1964, 92) and Jean-Paul Sartre (1976, 103) are only two of the Western writers to cite or describe this device.

A second major "Asian" element in Wilder's theatre—although less exclusively Asian than pantomime—is the frequent use of "found" or commonplace objects to suggest the outlines or basic structure of absent scenic elements. It is a device akin to pantomime—an object, such as a table, pretending to be something else, such as a cliff. Such "visual puns" are a notable feature of the Chinese stage, in particular, where a table and two chairs are almost the only stage properties needed. In a variety of ingenious ways, these humble items serve to represent the places and objects required for the action, from mountains and prison windows to garden walls and wells (Chen 1951, 28). In the *nô,* too, visual puns are occasionally employed. For instance, a cloth is used in *Taniko* (The Valley Rite) to represent a heap of stones and earth covering a dead boy, and in *Komachi and the Hundred Nights* a similar cloth represents a clump of grasses from which a ghost emerges. At the same time, however, scenic practices in the *nô,* while minimalistic and austere, tend to fall under the heading of "selective realism" or partial representation rather than symbolic substitution or visual metaphor. The few scenic properties used suggest, at least, the true, complete outlines of the objects they are supposed to represent. More to the point, they are obviously expressly constructed as theatrical properties, not "found" objects that in another context perform a different function. Huts or cottages are represented by small bamboo frameworks, but the bell in *Dojoji* is normally a realistic, full-size papier-mâché or cloth-and-wood reproduction. The one exception to this tendency is the fan, a ubiquitous hand property in both the *nô* and *kabuki,* which does represent a wide array of small objects, from serving trays and bottles to teacups, swords, knives, whips, pipes, and lanterns (Ernst 1974, 161). However, this convention of the Japanese stage has no especially close parallel in Wilder's plays, where hand properties are either realistic or imaginary.

Visual puns for Wilder are primarily scenic devices. Examples in *Our Town* include the stepladders that represent the upper floors of the Gibbs and Webb houses and the chairs and plank of lumber that create the drugstore soda fountain. One might also cite the chairs that serve as automobile seats in "The Happy Journey" and as passenger seats and berths in "Pullman Car" and the low stools that represent bushes in "Childhood," as well as the boxes of various sizes that represent rocks in the recently published one-act piece, "The Rivers under the Earth." All of these were probably inspired as much—or more—by children's make-believe games as by Asian stage conventions.

Other anti-illusionistic techniques are shared by Wilder's theatre and several of its Asian counterparts, though. The most immediately obvious and perhaps the most important of these techniques is the visible scene shift, accomplished in the Chinese and Japanese theatres by the technically "invisible" property man. Critics who refer to the Stage Manager in *Our Town* as a form of Chinese property man are only partially correct, however. At least one of them (Eaton 1938), in terming the Stage Manager a "vocal Chinese property man" (21), touches upon a crucial distinction. The difference lies in the respective functions of Wilder's Stage Manager and the property man. The latter essentially "disappears" while he is on stage, the audience being only marginally aware of his presence. His task is to assist with the mechanical aspects of the performance efficiently and, above all, unobtrusively. The Stage Manager in *Our Town* is meant to be anything but an "invisible," self-effacing assistant to the other performers. He not only serves as chorus and bit player but also shapes and controls the entire performance, responsibilities far beyond those assigned to the Asian property man. The same is true of the stage managers in Wilder's other minimalist dramas, too—Mr. Washburn in "Pullman Car Hiawatha" and the nameless man in "The Happy Journey." At the same time, Wilder does employ in *Our*

Town a reasonable facsimile of the property man: the stage assistants who, while the Stage Manager is meditating aloud to the audience about the wider significance of the action, accomplish the more extensive scene changes, such as the change from Main Street to the interior of the church in act 2.

A different Chinese theatrical convention directly inspired one specific scenic element in "The Long Christmas Dinner," too. That element is the pair of portals that Wilder uses to represent birth and death. According to the playwright, the idea derived from a standard feature of the Chinese stage: the two doorways in the upstage wall, one on the right side and one on the left (Simon 1979, 88). These doorways are known as "Spirit Doors," and entrances are generally made through the stage-right opening and exits through its stage-left counterpart (Arlington 1930, 26; Chen 1951, 21). Although the portals in "The Long Christmas Dinner" correspond fairly closely to these "Spirit Doors" in their placement ("birth" stage right, "death" stage left), Wilder goes beyond Chinese practice in assigning them symbolic meanings.

Beyond these techniques, conventions, or devices borrowed from or merely similar to Asian practices, Wilder's drama shares certain motifs with one particular Asian form, the *nô*. One such motif is that of the journey. In his July 1961 letter, he stated that the recurring device of the journey was one thing he would have borrowed from the *nô* had he been more familiar with it at the time he was writing his own plays (Wilder papers). He scarcely needed to borrow this device, for his *corpus* contains a quartet of "journey" plays: "Pullman Car Hiawatha," "The Happy Journey," "Childhood," and "The Flight into Egypt" (an early "three-minute play"). As in the *nô* repertory, the regular recurrence of the device carries symbolic weight and resonance. The traveler in *nô* dramas is usually a monk who, in many instances, receives a supernatural revelation at the end of his journey, which then becomes a process of discovery. Similarly, in Wilder's journey plays, the journey accompanies and in fact symbolizes an increase in awareness, whether of the wonders of the natural and supernatural worlds (as in "Pullman Car") or of the incalculable value of individual human beings (as in "The Happy Journey").

The other motif shared by Wilder's drama and the *nô* is that of the return to earth—and particularly to an emotionally compelling site—of a ghost or spirit. In the last act of *Our Town* Emily's compulsion to return to the familiar scenes of her earthly existence closely resembles the compulsion of the *nô* ghosts to reenact or recount the decisive moments of their lives. Wilder is certainly not making a Buddhist point in *Our Town* about the evils of earthly attachment—at least not consciously—and ghosts have been a staple of Western drama ever since Aeschylus, but the return of the deceased to an event from her life is decidedly closer to the *nô*.

Besides these features of Wilder's theatre, many other elements in his minimalist drama show a kinship with both Asian and Western traditional theatre. Most of these elements fall under the heading, again, of anti-illusionistic or theatricalist devices. Three of them, although not exclusively Asian, deserve comment here because they help complete the picture of the "Asian" aspects of Wilder's plays. The three elements are the intrusion of the action into the auditorium, the intrusion of everyday "reality" into the world of the play, and the assumption of female roles by male actors.

The resemblance between Wilder's theatre and Asian forms is weakest with respect to the last of these, but the connection is nevertheless worth noting and intriguing in its own right. The meticulous, essentially illusionistic female impersonation of the *dan* actor or *onnagata*— or of the Elizabethan boy actor, for that matter—would be out of place in Wilder's theatrical universe, but the stage managers in *Our Town,* "The Happy Journey," and "Pullman Car" are all obliged to play minor female characters at one point or another in their respective plays. Farthest from Asian practices in this area is the man in "The Happy Journey," who preserves a Brechtian distance from the roles he assumes by merely reading the lines of "Mrs. Hobmeyer" and other neighbors and friends of the family "with little attempt at characterization, scarcely troubling himself to alter his voice, even when he responds in the person of a child or a woman" (Wilder [1931] 1980, 86). All the same, Wilder's repeated use of the device in these three plays is suggestive. Even more intriguing is the report that the playwright toyed for a time with the idea of specifying that all roles in *The Skin of Our Teeth* be played by men (Harrison 1983, 217). It was in all likelihood the Greek, Elizabethan, and possibly medieval precedents that inspired Wilder to experiment with this device; but it must be remembered that Mei Lanfang specialized in *dan* roles, and Wilder's experiments in blurring the gender boundary link his theatre to Asian traditions as much as to European ones and thus help establish his work as a meeting point for East and West.

The same is true to an even greater extent of his penchant for breaching the fourth wall. His method of doing so most often involves bringing performers into the auditorium, whether as supposed spectators, as in act 1 of *Our Town,* or through the use of the theatre aisles, as in the wedding procession and recession in that play and the boarding of the "ark" in act 2 of *The Skin of Our Teeth.* Although the Western tradition—from *Fulgens and Lucrece* and *The Knight of the Burning Pestle* to the staging practices in the Spanish *corrales* and Pirandello's *Tonight We Improvise*—is rich in precedents for these "experiments" in mingling performers and spectators, at least two writers have noted the parallel between Wilder's use of the auditorium aisles as acting areas and the use of the *hanamichi* in *kabuki* (Ernst 1974, 66; Pronko 1967, 144–45).

The converse of the actors' "invasion" of the audience's territory, the intrusion of "reality" into the dramatic world, appears most spectacularly in Wilder's drama in *The Skin of Our Teeth*, where not only Sabina but also Antrobus, Henry, and Mrs. Antrobus all drop out of character in order to deal with various theatrical crises and interruptions as "themselves." As an unpublished "Note on Pirandello" by Wilder implies (Wilder papers), Luigi Pirandello may have served as the American dramatist's immediate inspiration for this assault on the theatrical illusion. However, Chinese opera performers, too, move between different levels of reality in performance. On their first entrance, they are not considered to be in character until they have sung the prologue for the next action, announced the name of the character they will be playing, and signaled the audience by lowering their arm from the "introduction sleeve" pose (Chen 1951, 38). Similarly, *kabuki* actors regularly break character in performance, whether to have perspiration wiped off their brows, sip a cup of tea, or have their costumes adjusted (Ernst 1974, 189). Ironically, Wilder is here the greater illusionist because his characters only appear to step outside their roles, whereas the *kabuki* performer actually does the deed. In *The Skin of Our Teeth*, the words spoken "out of character" are still the playwright's.

In a more elaborate and sophisticated form of juggling with actor/role ambiguities, actors in both Eastern and Western traditional theatres occasionally refer (or did refer) to their real selves while in character. For instance, the title character in the *kabuki* play *Narukami*, wishing to choose a new name for himself, settles on the performer's actual name; and in Webster's Induction to Marston's *The Malcontent*, Will Sly, one of the King's Men, appearing as a spectator on the stage, calls out the other members of the company and asks to see himself, whom he knows to be one of the troupe. Wilder never indulges in this sort of intricate theatricalist jesting, but the dual levels of action in *Skin* and other plays certainly point in the same direction, and the dramatist reportedly approved of director Alan Schneider's decision to have Mary Martin (Sabina) and other actors in his 1955 production of *The Skin of Our Teeth* call one another by their real names when they were "out of character" and refer to roles they had really played in other productions (Schneider 1986, 213). Even Wilder's use of pantomime, although inspired by a Chinese performer, can be seen as an area where East and West merge, for the device has been used in such Western traditions as the *commedia dell'arte*. In Carlo Gozzi's *The Green Bird,* for example, one even finds an extended *lazzo* involving a pantomimically created door.

That Wilder's theatre is a meeting place for a multitude of theatrical idioms from around the world and across the ages is no accident. Impressively erudite and multilingual and perennially obsessed with the problem of the individual's place in the cosmos, Wilder created an eclectic theatrical idiom of his own that draws together the furthest reaches of the theatrical "cosmos" in which it exists. Like W. B. Yeats he seems to have sought, consciously or subconsciously, to develop a style "that remembers many masters, that it may escape contemporary suggestion" (qtd. in Styan 1981, 64). Contemporary composer Alfred Schnittke coined the term "polystylistics" to describe his musical idiom, and the term aptly characterizes Wilder's dramatic style as well. In creating that style, Wilder also brought East and West a little closer together.

Works Cited

Arlington, L. C. 1930. *The Chinese Drama from the Earliest Times until Today.* Shanghai: Kelly and Walsh.

Benchley, Robert. 1938. "Two at Once. Review of *Our Town,* by Thornton Wilder." *New Yorker,* 12 February, 26.

Brecht, Bertolt. 1964. *Brecht on Theatre: The Development of an Aesthetic.* Ed. and trans. John Willett. New York: Hill and Wang.

Burbank, Rex. 1961. *Thornton Wilder.* Twayne's United States Authors Series, no. 5. New Haven: College and University Press.

Chen, Jack. 1951. *The Chinese Theatre.* New York: Roy.

Eastman, Fred. 1938. "The Pulitzer Prize Drama. Review of *Our Town,* by Thornton Wilder." *Christian Century,* 3 August, 943–44.

Eaton, Walter Prichard. 1938. "Review of *Our Town,* by Thornton Wilder." *New York Herald Tribune Books,* 1 May, 21.

Ernst, Earle. [1956] 1974. *The Kabuki Theatre.* Honolulu: University of Hawaii Press.

Haberman, Donald. 1967. *The Plays of Thornton Wilder: A Critical Study.* Middletown: Wesleyan University Press.

Harrison, Gilbert A. 1983. *The Enthusiast: A Life of Thornton Wilder.* New Haven: Ticknor and Fields.

Keene, Donald, ed. 1970. *Twenty Plays of the Nō Theatre.* New York: Columbia University Press.

Pronko, Leonard. 1967. *Theater East and West: Perspectives Toward a Total Theater.* Berkeley: University of California Press.

Raghavan, V. 1981. "Sanskrit Drama in Performance." In *Sanskrit Drama in*

Performance, ed. Rachel Van M. Baumer and James R. Brandon. Honolulu: University of Hawaii Press.

Sartre, Jean-Paul. 1976. *Sartre on Theatre.* Ed. Michel Contat and Michel Rybalka. Translated by Frank Jellinek. New York: Random House/Pantheon.

Schneider, Alan. 1986. *Entrances: An American Director's Journey.* New York: Viking.

Simon, Linda. 1979. *Thornton Wilder: His World.* Garden City: Doubleday.

Styan, J. L. 1981. *Symbolism, Surrealism, and the Absurd.* Vol. 2, *Modern Drama in Theory and Practice.* Cambridge: Cambridge University Press.

Wilder, Thornton. [1931] 1980. "The Happy Journey to Trenton and Camden." In *The Long Christmas Dinner and Other Plays in One Act.* New York: Avon/Bard.

———. Papers. Beinecke Rare Book and Manuscript Library, Yale University.

Who Speaks and Authorizes?

The Aftermath of Brecht's Misinterpretation
of the Classical Chinese Theatre

Min Tian

*I*N THE LANDSCAPE of twentieth-century intercultural theatre, Bertolt Brecht stands as a symbolic figure for having forged an aesthetic that incorporates Asian traditions, especially those of the classical Chinese theatre. Moreover, his interpretation and use of the classical Chinese theatre have provided in return a rationale for the Chinese reevaluation of their own traditional theatre and a model for their avant-garde experiments in spoken drama, supported by their productions of Brecht's plays. Brecht's essay "Alienation Effects in Chinese Acting" (1964) has been hailed, especially in China, for its "deep insight" into the classical Chinese theatre. Elsewhere (Tian 1997) I have demonstrated that it was not in Chinese acting that Brecht found his "A-effect," nor does Chinese acting confirm Brecht's theory. Chinese acting does not in fact generate anything even similar to the A-effect. Brecht clearly made use of the Chinese theatre to validate and legitimize his own theoretical desires, investments, and projections; his essay is essentially a highly subjective elaboration of his own theory.

Ironically, in the 1950s, when Brecht's interpretation of the classical Chinese theatre appeared in China, it significantly affected the Chinese view of and confidence in their own theatrical tradition. Brecht's view attracted many supporters, most of whom took pride in his appraisal of their indigenous tradition without questioning its validity. In this article I shall first examine how Brecht's views affected the Chinese attitude toward their own theatrical tradition and then assess this phenomenon in a historical perspective. That perspective entails examination of the intercultural exchanges of the present century affecting the Chinese view of and confidence in their own theatrical tradition in varying degrees. This transpired in response to such sharply contrasting Western theories as those of Brecht and Stanislavsky.

Huang Zuolin, one of the most influential theatre artists in contemporary China, has contributed significantly to the Chinese reception of Brecht's epic theatre. Huang's interest in Brecht's theory was stimulated by Brecht's essay on the Chinese theatre, for it inspired him with "great national pride" (Huang 1982b, 96) in the classical Chinese theatre, as he acknowledged: "I feel quite ashamed that, as a Chinese theatre artist, I was no more than an enthusiastic spectator of our nation's classical theatre art and did not make a deep and systematic study of it. It can even be said that it was Brecht's essay that aroused my interest in Chinese classical theatre art" (Huang 1982a, 256). In the English version of Huang's article, this passage was cut (see Huang 1982b, 98), yet it is clear that Brecht's misinterpretation strongly influenced Huang. Indeed, Huang accepted Brecht's views with uncritical admiration, and he wrote a supplement to Brecht's essay, endorsing Brecht's "deep insight" into the Chinese theatre, only pointing out certain "inaccurate observation[s]" of "no importance" (see Huang 1982b).

Huang's validation of Brecht's misinterpretation is instrumental in his mistaken assertion that the classical Chinese theatre is anti-illusionist. In fact, the classical Chinese theatre is essentially a theatre of "illusion." But whereas naturalistic illusion is achieved by detailed physical decor and imitation of daily life and behavior, classical Chinese theatre creates illusion primarily by the performer's stylistic gestures and movements. That of course requires audience imagination, and it also produces a powerful effect of empathy rather than critical alienation in the mind of the spectator. Huang's view of the classical Chinese theatre is actually a strange combination of Brecht's and Stanislavsky's ideas. For instance, he interpreted Wang Xiaonong's (1858–1918) portrayal of the drunken poet, Li Bai, in this way: "[The] upper part of the body thoroughly and completely impersonated the drunken poet, but the lower part played the horse who [*sic*] is sober and steady. Thus may we not say that the upper part is in the style of Stanislavsky, while the lower part is Brechtian? When both the upper and lower parts are put together it is wholly Chinese traditional theatre" (Huang 1990, 184).

I do not question that Huang's binary mutilation of Wang's body can do justice to Wang's performance as an organic whole, but it seems to me that in Huang's interpretation the true identity and unique characteristics of Wang's performance (and Chinese performance as well) was lost, or, more precisely, displaced.

Like Huang, A Jia, a leading director in contemporary China, also maintained that traditional Chinese theatre, which dispenses with the "fourth wall," is nonillusionist and produces the "A-effect." For example, regarding one of the performance conventions, *dabeigong* (aside), A Jia asserted that "no other method than this one gives more prominence to the 'A-effect' " (A Jia 1983, 447). But considering that the convention of the *dabeigong* calls for the performer to raise his hand and hide his face from one side to suggest that his speech is not heard by other characters on stage, it seems to me that the convention is designed emphatically to create stage illusion, not otherwise. All theatre depends on convention. In naturalistic theatre, asides are eliminated in accordance with the fourth wall convention, whereas the classical Chinese theatre keeps the spirit of illusion alive by other means.

Be that as it may, the introduction of Brecht's ideas into China, especially his misinterpretation of the classical Chinese theatre and Huang's endorsement of them, led to increased production of his plays and inspired new approaches to traditional Chinese plays. The first of Brecht's plays to appear on the Chinese stage was *Mother Courage and Her Children*, directed by Huang Zuolin at the Shanghai People's Art Theatre in 1959. According to the set designer, Gong Boan, the set was a combination of the design used at the Berliner Ensemble and that of the classical Chinese theatre. What underpinned the use of traditional Chinese theatre was Huang's conviction that Brecht represented a revived and valid form of traditional Chinese theatre. Huang gave a lecture before the rehearsals of the play began in which he concluded that the Chinese should learn from Brecht's use of the Chinese theatre because the basic characteristic of classical Chinese theatre, conventionality, is identical with Brecht's A-effect (Huang 1959, 19–20). In the same vein Gong Boan stated: "Brecht's borrowing of the artistic principles from Chinese opera gave us in return constructive assistance during our rehearsals of his plays. This was seen in the whole process of search for the meaning of the alienation effect during the rehearsals" (Gong 1982, 66).

Twenty years later the 1979 production of *Life of Galileo* at the Chinese Youth Art Theatre, directed by Huang Zuolin and Chen Yong, was hailed as a landmark experiment of nonillusionist performance in the modern Chinese theatre. Xue Dianjie, the designer, declared that he used certain principles of spatial treatment from the classical Chinese theatre in his design, convinced that "the traditional Chinese theatre, such as Peking Opera and other regional theatres, is basically anti-illusionistic in its treatment of acting space" (Xue 1982, 75) and that "Brecht's epic theatre (or 'narrative theatre') is similar to our traditional theatre as far as anti-illusionism ('removal of illusion') is concerned" (Xue 1982, 80).

In contrast to these two productions, *The Good Person of Setzuan* was adapted and presented in a complete regional theatrical form, *chuanju* (Sichuan song-dance theatre). This production was initiated by Ding Yangzhong, a Brecht specialist. The reasoning undergirding Ding's conception was again Brecht's interest in and his use of the Chinese theatre. Like Huang, Ding insisted that Brecht had found in the Chinese theatre "the object of his search": an ideal performance style and theatrical form he could apply to his own theatre (Ding 1990, 171). For Ding, because Brecht's test of the Chinese theatre in his own theatre resulted in "a revolutionary performance art," the Chinese undoubtedly could follow suit and "reap the interest of our loan" (Ding, 171). The production was well received. A German scholar, Ernst Schumacher, observed that it was the best performance of a Brecht play he had seen for more than ten years (Ding, 176). A Chinese reviewer, however, while praising the production as a cross-fertilizing experiment, noted that one of the failures of the production was its deliberate overemphasis on the Alienation-effect, which interfered with and impeded the spectator's normal thinking and appreciation (Yi 1987). For instance, there were actors' collective exercises at the beginning of the production and the property men's martial arts at intervals, which were added to produce the A-effect. In my opinion the reason for such failures resides precisely in the underlying misconception that the classical Chinese theatre, like Sichuan opera, features the Brechtian A-effect and in the production's undue capitalization on it.

Spoken drama was imported into China from the West in the early twentieth century as part of a revolt against traditional theatre launched by a generation of radical intellectuals in the May Fourth Movement. In recent decades spoken drama has been undergoing a deep crisis. In response to the impact of Orientalism in Western theatre, especially Brecht's use of the classical Chinese theatre, Chinese theatre artists turned to their own theatre's past to revitalize spoken drama by incorporating traditional techniques and principles of presentation. Some of the resulting plays produced in the 1980s and 1990s, notably *Zhongguo Meng* (China Dream) and *Sangshuping Jishi* (The Story of the Mulberry Village), seem to have opened new vistas in contemporary Chinese theatre.

China Dream, written by Sun Huizhu and Fei Chunfang and directed by Huang Zuolin, was first produced in Shanghai in 1987. According to the authors, like many Chinese spoken drama artists, they were inspired by Brecht and other Western theatre artists' interest in Chinese and Asian theatres in their exploration into "the possibilities of integrating some more expressive styles of sung drama into spoken

drama" (Sun and Fei 1996, 189). According to Huang Zuolin the production of *China Dream* purported to be his experiment of "a cohesion
of the Stanislavsky, Brecht, and Mei Lanfang philosophies of theatrical
art" (Huang 1990, 184). Some techniques and elements from traditional
Chinese performance were used in the production to produce alienation
effects in the Brechtian sense.

Unlike Huang Zuolin, who was inspired directly by Brecht, Xu
Xiaozhong, director of *The Story of the Mulberry Village* and one of the
leading directors in China today, was trained in Russia and launched his
career as an enthusiastic advocate of the Stanislavsky system. In the
1980s, however, Xu turned to Brecht and the classical Chinese theatre
and sought for a fusion of their principles and Stanislavsky's. Xu noted
that Brecht, Meyerhold, Grotowski, and others found inspiration in
traditional Chinese theatre to help them break away from the confines
of illusionism and rediscover the essence of theatre. He bemoaned the
fact that for too long Chinese theatre artists had looked on nineteenth-
century European illusionism as the essence of spoken drama (Xu 1982,
382–83). Clearly, Xu felt a kinship with Brecht and other Western theatre
artists, but unlike Brecht and Huang, Xu integrated the aesthetic of
traditional Chinese theatre not for its supposed anti-illusionist A-effect
but for its "poetic association and atmospheric illusion" characterized
by him as "poeticized imagery" (Xu 1988, 413). These qualities are essentially imaginary and spiritual and thus very different from the European illusionist pursuit of physical verisimilitude. Xu's experiment is
best exemplified in his production of *The Story of the Mulberry Village*.
Xu notes that in applying Brecht's theory people tend to overstress the
significance of intellect at the expense of emotion, resulting in a cold
and detached attitude on the part of the spectator. Xu argues that traditional Chinese theatre stresses the fusion of emotion and intellect,
and he considers such a principle instrumental as an alternative (Xu 1988,
410). In contrast to Huang's, Xu's view appears closer to the Chinese
theatre.

Paradoxically, Brecht's misinterpretation of the classical Chinese
theatre has had both negative and positive effects in the aftermath of
its appearance in China. On the one hand, it has misled many Chinese
theatre artists to a misconception of their traditional theatre; on the
other, it has helped to strengthen and renew the Chinese confidence in
their theatrical tradition and to enrich and renovate contemporary Chinese theatre by drawing on Brecht's appropriation of their own theatrical tradition. But negative or positive notwithstanding, it seems to me
that this phenomenon should be seen and assessed historically in the

perspective of the intercultural theatrical exchange between China and the West.

It is well known that during the May Fourth Movement in the first decade of the twentieth century, many radical intellectuals influenced by Western realism repudiated traditional Chinese theatre. They deplored the lack of social ideals in traditional Chinese theatre, the rigidity of its conventions, the absurdity of its makeup, the simplicity of its stage equipment, and the artificiality and decadence of its female impersonation. Some demanded that the traditional theatre be made to conform to Western realist theatre in order to meet the necessity of social and political reform. As a result several plays called *shizhuang xinxi* (new plays in modern costumes) appeared using realistic scenery, costumes, and electric light in traditional theatrical performances. Most of these new plays were produced at the Shanghai New Stage, the first modern theatre with a proscenium in China. Even Mei Lanfang, under the influence of a few theatre artists who were familiar with Western realist theatre, performed in a number of plays in the style of *shizhuang xinxi*. In these performances, according to Mei, stylized performance conventions were replaced by realistic movements and gestures; singing was reduced and more speech added; costumes and properties were also made realistic (for example, a real sewing machine was put on stage) (Mei 1957, 3–4). A few years later, however, Mei gave up such experiments, realizing that realistic movements and gestures were incompatible with the dance movements and performance techniques of Beijing Opera (Mei 1957, 70). What was condemned as nonrealistic and was subject to realist reform was precisely what European avant-garde artists, such as Meyerhold, Eisenstein, and Brecht, found useful in the classical Chinese theatre in their campaign against the nineteenth-century naturalist tradition and what the Chinese, following their examples, are now trying to reevaluate.

During the 1950s, when the Stanislavsky "system" was formally accepted as orthodoxy in Chinese theatrical circles, remarkable efforts were made either to identify and theorize on Stanislavskian elements in the classical Chinese theatre—such as the performer's inner experience of the character portrayed, the "magic if," "given circumstances," "through action," "super-objective," and so forth—or to reform it in accordance with the Stanislavsky system. As early as 1957, A Jia, one of the first specialists of the classical Chinese theatre who became familiar with Stanislavsky's theory, pointed out that many Chinese theatre artists who hoped to resolve problems in the classical Chinese theatre started not from the reality of the classical Chinese theatre but from certain doctrines, replacing the forms of expression of the classical Chinese theatre with naturalism (A Jia 1957, 119). In January 1958, at the conference of the All-China Theatre Workers' Association, a discussion was devoted to how to apply the Stanislavsky system to classical Chinese theatre, and a number of scenes taken from Beijing operas were performed in the Stanislavsky manner. After the event a Russian specialist, G. N. Gureev, was asked to give a speech on the subject. Gureev asserted that many basic principles of the Stanislavsky system could be found in the classical Chinese theatre and that they were used in a more exquisite manner (Gureev 1958, 107). It is not surprising that Gureev's view was accepted by many Chinese artists who were eager to defend their indigenous theatre by associating it with a supposedly scientific system. Li Zigui, a noted performer and director of the classical Chinese theatre, had two articles devoted to the ongoing debate on the relationship between the classical Chinese theatre and the Stanislavsky system (Li 1957, 345–61; 1958, 362–74). Li argued that the classical Chinese theatre has all the elements of the Stanislavsky system, although the terms used are different and no one in the Chinese theatre had yet fully analyzed these elements into a systematic theory. Thus, for Li the Stanislavsky system can not only help Chinese artists understand the "secrets of success" in their performances, raising them to the level of "a scientific theory," but also aid in improving the classical Chinese theatre in practice. After tenacious explorations and experiments for five decades, however, Li realized that it is not feasible to apply Stanislavsky to performance of classical Chinese theatre, for the integration of the system into classical Chinese theatre must allow for their differences in the first place. He acknowledged that there were "some welding traces" (Li 1990, 590) in his wedding the Stanislavsky system to the classical Chinese theatre.

Jiao Juyin, considered the most important and influential Stanislavsky specialist in China, attempted to apply Stanislavsky acting methods to the performance of Beijing Opera (Jiao 1957, 113). Jiao argued that classical Chinese theatre and the Stanislavsky system are compatible, insisting that "the performance art of traditional Chinese theatre belongs to the category of the school of experiencing" (Jiao 1959, 327) and that "in its basic principles, the performance art of traditional Chinese theatre coincides with his [Stanislavsky's] system" (Jiao 1959, 328). But later Jiao apparently changed or compromised his view. In a lecture delivered in 1963 on how to learn from the classical Chinese theatre, Jiao quoted Brecht's list of contrasting differences between the "dramatic form of theatre" and the "epic form of theatre" and then stated that Brecht adopted a great deal from the Chinese theatre. He assumed that if

Brecht had come to China, "he must have found in our traditional theatre a more profound and precise aesthetic foundation for his theory and practice" (Jiao 1963, 282). In China in the middle of the 1960s the Stanislavsky system was officially condemned as idealistic, and enthusiasm was already shifting to Brecht. It was under these circumstances that Jiao argued, in a talk given in 1964 on the reformation of the classical Chinese theatre, that "it is not right to apply the Stanislavsky system indiscriminately to Chinese traditional theatrical art and to use it as a criterion of interpreting the experience of Chinese traditional theatrical art, . . . for Chinese aesthetic idea, habit, and psychology are totally different from those of the West" (Jiao 1964, 29).

It is noteworthy that, unlike Huang, before his exposure to Stanislavsky's and Brecht's theories, Jiao had already gained a solid grasp of the classical Chinese theatre during his presidency in a classical Chinese drama school. Later in his career, Jiao engaged vigorously and consistently in a campaign for the nationalization of spoken drama, which purported to draw on the traditional theatre. It is nevertheless unquestionable that Jiao's interpretation and use of the classical Chinese theatre were influenced by Stanislavsky's and, to a lesser degree, Brecht's theories.

Finally, Mei Lanfang's response to the Stanislavsky impact bears examination. According to Mei, Stanislavsky's stress on "relaxation," "through action," and "subconsciousness" in performance is commensurate with the performance experiences of Chinese *xiqu* performers, including his own (Mei 1959, 204). Mei stated that he wanted to apply Stanislavsky's system properly to the classical Chinese theatre so that Chinese traditional performance art could be strenghtened with "new nourishment." In his view, the legacy of the classical Chinese theatre is in need of a complete systematization in a "scientific approach" in light of Stanislavsky's theory (Mei 1959, 205). Mei did not propose a mechanical copy of Stanislavsky's method; however, his view clearly partook of the general sense of inferiority on the part of many Chinese theatre artists chagrined that classical Chinese theatre lacks "a scientific system."

Aside from Stanislavsky's and Brecht's theories, Denis Diderot's eighteenth-century idea of acting had a bearing on the Chinese interpretation of their traditional theatre. In 1961 Zhu Guangqian, a noted scholar, published an article on Diderot's *Paradox of the Actor* in the leading official newspaper, *Renmin Ribao* (People's Daily). Zhu's article elicited great enthusiasm and interest among theatre artists, and the Chinese Theatre Artists' Association held two symposia on the issue. In his article Zhu maintains that compared with other theories of acting, Diderot's is "closer to the truth" (Zhu 1961). He relates Diderot's theory to Chinese traditional acting, arguing that "the practice of the performers of traditional Chinese theatre agrees with Diderot's requirements. . . . Chinese traditional performers are truly Diderot's ideal actors. . . . [I]ndeed, they [Chinese performers] perform according to a prescribed 'ideal type' " (Zhu 1961). It is true that the highly conventionalized performance style of traditional Chinese theatre with its relatively fixed gestures and movements may bear superficial resemblance to Diderot's "ideal type" of acting; however, in traditional Chinese acting the performer indeed has an intense emotional experience of, and identification with, the character portrayed (Tian 1997), and these are incompatible with Diderot's theory of acting, which allows no sensibility and emotion to the actor. But what is more problematic in Zhu's association of Chinese acting with Diderot's theory is the premise of his judgment: if Chinese acting had not been fortunate enough to agree with Diderot's requirements, it would not have been scientific or closer to the truth.

In the foregoing I have examined the historical fact that different and contrasting Western theatrical theories have strongly affected the Chinese attitude toward their own indigenous theatre. In the history of intercultural communication between China and the West, the aftermath of Brecht's misinterpretation of the classical Chinese theatre epitomized a profoundly ironic situation. The Self was defined and enriched by the Other, not through a true understanding of the Other but through a nexus of misconceptions and misguided endorsements. Although those misconceptions and endorsements (imaginary or creative) proved fruitful in artistic experiments, they also proved destructive in that they displaced the true identity of the Other (the Chinese tradition) and thereby muddied our understanding of its true essence. Brecht's misinterpretation and its Chinese endorsement provide a profound lesson: true intercultural theatre should be based on a true understanding of the Other, which does not necessarily kill imagination and creativity. Imaginary or creative misconception and appropriation of the Other could never become truly cross-fertilizing and productive because of their destructive effects on the Other. Perhaps the biggest irony in all this is that Chinese confidence in their own traditional theatre needed to be nourished by the authorization, even if mistaken, of a supposedly superior or "scientific" theory from the West. It led them to undertake innovations and experimentation even based on their acceptance of misconceptions about their own tradition.

Thus, given the positive impact of intercultural theatre on contemporary Chinese theatre, there is no denying that what is valid, legitimate, superior, scientific, or universal is determined primarily not by the essence and value of the theatre (primarily the Eastern) concerned but by a hierarchical, recentralized, socially and economically charged structure of discourse: who speaks and authorizes. In such a discourse the Other is not in a position to speak for itself and to determine the nature and outcome of the exchange but is subject to endorsing and subscribing to a privileged authority, even a mistaken one, who has what Edward Said calls the "flexible positional superiority" (Said 1978, 7) of speaking for the Other. Said defines "Orientalism" as "a Western style for dominating, restructuring, and having authority over the Orient," and he further notes that "because of Orientalism, the Orient was not (and is not) a free subject of thought and action" (3). Thus, the Oriental Other is brought to recognize and appreciate the Orientalist judgment on and use of things Oriental either through domination on the part of the Occident or by consent and valorization on the part of the Orient. Said's observation can apply with equal force to Brecht's misinterpretation of the classical Chinese theatre and its endorsement by the Chinese. Such a discourse determined that there was no and would be no intercultural theatre truly worthy of its name. Richard Schechner's "Utopia dream" of intercultural theatre—"to have difference which is chosen and which is culture-specific, without it necessarily being hierarchical and authoritarian" (Schechner 1996, 50)—is worth dreaming of, but its materialization can become a possibility only when the necessity that "the exchange . . . be on the basis of equivalence," as Schechner has realized (1996, 48), has truly become a reality.

Works Cited

A Jia. 1957. "Shenghuo de zhengshi he *xiqu* biaoyan yishu de zhengshi" (The truth of life and the truth of the performance art of the classical Chinese theatre). Reprinted in *Xiqu biaoyan yishu lun ji* (Essays on the performance art of the classical Chinese theatre), 119–43. Shanghai: Shanghai Wenyi Chubanshe, 1962, 1979.

———. 1983. "*Xiqu* daoyan" (Directing in the classical Chinese theatre). In *Zhongguo dabaikequanshu: xiqu he quyi* (China's encyclopedia: *xiqu* and *quyi*), ed. Zhongguo Dabaikequanshu Bianjibu. Beijing: Zhongguo Dabaikequanshu Chubanshe.

Brecht, Bertolt. 1964. "Alienation Effects in Chinese Acting." In *Brecht on Theatre*, ed. and trans. John Willett, 91–99. New York: Hill and Wang.

Ding Yangzhong. 1990. "On the Insatiable Appetite and Longevity of Theatre." In *The Dramatic Touch of Difference: Theatre Foreign and Own*, ed. Erika Fischer Lichte, Josephine Riley, and Michael Gissenwehrer, 169–77. Tubingen Gunter Narr Verlag.

Gong Boan. 1982. "First Performance of Brecht's Dramatic Work in China— the Production of *Mother Courage* and Its Stage Design." In *Brecht and East Asian Theatre,* ed. Antony Tatlow and Tak-Wai Wong, 65–71. Hong Kong: Hong Kong University Press.

Gureev, G. N. 1958. "Zhongguo *xiqu* yu Sitannisilafusiji tixi" (The classical Chinese theatre and the Stanislavsky system). *Xiju Lunzun* (Essays on theatre) no. 1.

Huang Zuolin. 1959. "Guanyu Deguo *xiju* yishujia Bulaixite" (About German theatre artist Brecht). Reprinted in *Lun Bulaixite xiju yishu* (Essays on Brecht's theatrical art), ed. Zhongguo Xiju Chubanshe Bianjibu, 1–21. Beijing: Zhongguo Xiju Chubanshe, 1984.

———. 1982a. "Bulaixite 'Zhongguo *xiju* yishu zhong de moshenghua xiaoguo' du hou buchong" (A supplement to Brecht's 'Alienation Effects in Chinese Acting'). Reprinted in *Lun Bulaixite xiju yishu,* 255–66.

———. 1982b. "A Supplement to Brecht's 'Alienation Effects in Chinese Acting.' " In *Brecht and East Asian Theatre,* ed. Antony Tatlow and Tak-Wai Wong, 96–110. Hong Kong: Hong Kong University Press.

———. 1990. " 'China Dream': A Fruition of Global Interculturalism." In *The Dramatic Touch of Difference: Theatre Foreign and Own,* ed. Erika Fischer Lichte, Josephine Riley, and Michael Gissenwehrer, 179–86. Gunter Narr Verlag.

Jiao Juyin. 1957. "Guanyu *huaju* xiqu *xiqu* biaoyan shoufa wenti" (On spoken drama's incorporation of the performance methods of the classical Chinese theatre). Reprinted in *Jiao Juyin xiju lunwen ji* (Jiao Juyin's essays on theatre), ed. Chen Gang, 113–24. Shanghai: Shanghai Wenyi Chubanshe, 1979.

———. 1959. "Lüe lun *huaju* de minzu xingshi he minzu fengge" (On spoken drama's national form and national style). Reprinted in *Jiao Juyin xiju lunwen ji* (Jiao Juyin's essays on theatre), ed. Chen Gang, 323–57. Shanghai: Shanghai Wenyi Chubanshe, 1979.

———. 1963. "Baotou, xiongyao, fengwei" (Leopard's head, bear's loins, and phoenix's tail). Reprinted in *Jiao Juyin xiju lunwen ji* (Jiao Juyin's essays on theatre), ed. Chen Gang, 273–97. Shanghai: Shanghai Wenyi Chubanshe, 1979.

———. 1964. "Tan *xiqu* gaige de jige wenti" (On some problems in the reformation of the classical Chinese theatre). Reprinted in *Jiao Juyin xiju sanlun* (Jiao Juyin's miscellaneous writings on theatre), ed. Du Dengfu, Jiang Rui, and Zhang Fan, 28–36. Beijing: Zhongguo Xiju Chubanshe, 1985.

Li Zigui. 1957. "*Xiqu* biaoyan de wutai zhengshi" (Stage truth in the performance of the classical Chinese theatre). Reprinted in *Li Zigui xiqu biaodaoyan yishu lun ji* (Li Zigui's essays on acting and directing of the classical Chinese theatre), ed. Liu Naichong, 345–61. Beijing: Zhongguo Xiju Chubanshe, 1992.

———. 1958. "Shitan Sitannisilafusiji tixi yu *xiqu* biaoyan yishu de guanxi" (A tentative discussion on the relationship between the Stanislavsky system and the performance art of the classical Chinese theatre). Reprinted in *Li Zigui xiqu biaodaoyan yishu lun ji* (Li Zigui's essays on acting and directing of the classical Chinese theatre), ed. Liu Naichong, 362–74. Beijing: Zhongguo Xiju Chubanshe, 1992.

———. 1990. "Houji" (Postscript). In *Li Zigui xiqu biaodaoyan yishu lun ji* (Li Zigui's essays on acting and directing of the classical Chinese theatre), ed. Liu Naichong, 585–94. Beijing: Zhongguo Xiju Chubanshe, 1992.

Mei Lanfang. 1957. *Wutai Shenghuo Sishinian* (Forty years of life on the stage). Vol. 2. Beijing: Renmin Wenxue Chubanshe.

———. 1959. "Huiyi Stannisilafusiji he Niemiluoweiqi-Danqinke" (In memory of Stanislavsky and Nemirovich-Danchenko). In *Mei Lanfang Xiju Sanlun* (Mei Lanfang's miscellaneous writings on theatre). Beijing: Zhongguo Xiju Chubanshe.

Said, Edward. 1978. *Orientalism*. New York: Pantheon Books.

Schechner, Richard. 1996. "Interculturalism and the Culture of Choice: Richard Schechner Interviewed by Patrice Pavis." In *The Intercultural Performance Reader*, ed. Patrice Pavis, 41–50. London: Routledge.

Sun, William, and Faye Fei. 1996. "*China Dream:* A Theatrical Dialogue between East and West." In *The Intercultural Performance Reader*, ed. Patrice Pavis, 188–95. London: Routledge.

Tian, Min. 1997. " 'Alienation-Effect' for Whom? Brecht's (Mis)interpretation of the Classical Chinese Theatre." *Asian Theatre Journal* 14, no. 2 (fall): 200–222.

Toshio, Kawatake. 1990. "Collision, or Point of Contact Between the 'Hanamichi' and the Western Theatre Tradition." In *The Dramatic Touch of Difference: Theatre Foreign and Own*, ed. Erika Fischer Lichte, Josephine Riley, and Michael Gissenwehrer, 99–105. Gunter Narr Verlag.

Xu Xiaozhong. 1982. "Ba ziji de xingshi fuyu ziji de guannian" (Integrating one's own form with one's own idea). Reprinted in *Xu Xiaozhong daoyan yishu yanjiu* (Studies in Xu Xiaozhong's art of directing), ed. Lin Yinyu, 381–88. Beijing: Zhongguo Xiju Chubanshe, 1991.

———. 1988. "Zai jianrong yu jiehe zhong shanbian: *huaju Sangshuping jishi* shiyan baogao" (Transmutation in incorporation: report on the experiment of *The Story of the Mulberry Village*). Reprinted in *Xu Xiaozhong daoyan yishu yanjiu* (Studies in Xu Xiaozhong's art of directing), ed. Lin Yinyu, 405–20. Beijing: Zhongguo Xiju Chubanshe, 1991.

Xue Dianjie. 1982. "Stage Design for Brecht's *Life of Galileo*." In *Brecht and East Asian Theatre*, ed. Antony Tatlow and Tak-Wai Wong, 72–87. Hong Kong: Hong Kong University Press.

Yi, Kai. 1987. "Yonggande jieshou Bulaixite de 'tiaozhan': *chuanju Sichuan haoren* guanhou" (Bravely accept Brecht's 'challenge': a review of *chuanju The Good Person of Sezuan*). *Wenyi Bao* (Literature and art report) 31 (October).

Zhu Guangqian. 1961. "Dideluo de *Tan yanyuan maodun*" (Diderot's *Paradox of the Actor*). *Renmin Ribao* (People's daily) 2 (February).

Great Reckonings

in a Simulated City

Artaud's Misunderstanding
of Balinese Theatre

Evan Winet

*I*N MUCH RECENT intercultural theatre practice, the distinctions once fundamental to modern primitivism have broken down. It becomes increasingly difficult to distinguish sacred from commercial practices. Victor Turner's distinction between the liminal practice of ritual and the liminoid practice of theatre is continually debated in capitalistic "commercial" cultures (see Turner 1982). John and Jean Comaroff have criticized the Eurocentric opposition of sacred ritual and secular modernity, demonstrating that ritual practices permeate modern Western life and that all cultures experience distinct forms of modernity (1993, xi–xxxvii). Western audiences have increasing access to diverse performance forms whose conventions they cannot read, and so they develop strategies for misreading those conventions. Theatrical reception becomes touristic. Interculturalism flourishes through a hermeneutic circle in which each disoriented reading produces new misunderstandings. Many of these misunderstandings actually form the basis for new artistic and intercultural forms. Naturally such transformations complicate any easy linear developmental narrative. Consequently, the logic of the avant-garde in the West becomes tenuous as do claims to cultural authenticity or purity in the East.

Artaud wrote about the Balinese theatre during the 1930s, the formative years of contemporary intercultural performance but also the declining years of overt performance of European colonialism. Christopher Innes places Artaud's writings on the Balinese in the context of colonial primitivism. In doing so he reverses strictly colonial logic and yet preserves the evolutionary notion of the Asian "others" as primitive reflections of a European past (1993, 12–18; see also Bharucha 1990, 14–17). Colonial apologists saw "children" in need of education, whereas primitivists saw "noble savages" before the Fall; both simplified their objects into ahistorical "traditional" cultures.

Artaud interpreted the Balinese theatre through a primitivist ideology. He did not, however, simply misunderstand the Balinese theatre, because the performance he witnessed at the Dutch pavilion of the Paris Colonial Exposition of 1931 was not simply Balinese theatre. The dancers participated in an experimental event developed jointly by Western and Balinese cultural authorities. The troupe appeared in a performance space designed to satisfy the colonial interests of the Dutch government. This stage occupied a small corner of a lavish Parisian Exposition celebrating the accomplishments of European colonialism. Because of this context native ritual naturally called for a performance environment closer to a postmodern Epcot Center than to either a Western stage or an Eastern village. Artaud's interpretation of the Balinese performance indicates his own ideological investment in Orientalism and colonialism. Nevertheless, these filters allowed him to engage creatively with an unfamiliar culture, producing writings on the Balinese theatre that even some Balinese scholars have admired (see Bandem and deBoer 1995). Thus, he did not simply misunderstand Balinese theatre. He allowed himself to experience the colonial exposition as a whole and subsequently reframed his experience as purely "Balinese."

In his essay "On the Balinese Theatre" Artaud assumes that the spectacle he witnessed was the product of the unifying vision of a director. Strictly speaking, no such figure existed for Balinese village performances. It is true, of course, that many "directors" choreographed the Exposition. Marshal Lyautey, an influential leader of French colonialism who had recently returned from Indochina, served as the overall director or administrator. In a manifesto printed in *Nineteenth Century and After*, he outlines a didactic mission for the Colonial Exposition. He hopes the Exposition will show the great Western nations "the work of awakening primitive or backward peoples to a more lively feeling for the dignity of man, of bringing to them more material welfare, and of raising them to a clearer recognition of the solidarity which, whether they wish it or not, binds together mankind" (1931, 538–39). Lyautey rationalizes the Exposition as a site for learning, exploration, and discovery in accordance with a colonial ideology that, apart from secularization, had not fundamentally changed since the sixteenth century. He concludes his statement by urging that the Exposition be viewed as "a point of departure" for greater colonial activity.

Victor Turner might well have described Lyautey's heuristic as liminoid. Artaud, however, experienced the Balinese performance at the Exposition liminally, as a metaphysically transformative ritual with the capacity to alter the nature of nature itself. He inverts Lyautey's colonial ideology into a primitivist one. The Balinese theatre reawakened in him a lively feeling for the power of theatre. It inspired a glimpse into "the hieroglyphic actor," which he incorporated into his Theatre of Cruelty. This concept has inspired a great many Dionysian happenings since his death, yet it began with a fundamental misunderstanding. His theatrical vision itself was metaphysical and immediate and, at the same time, mimetic and representational; as such, it was also impossible. In his essay "The Theatre of Cruelty and the Closure of Representation" Jacques Derrida brilliantly unravels this impossibility. Artaud, through a basically Platonic ideology, despised the difference between signs and their signified as well as the distance between self and representation. When he denounced God, he implicated all human institutions as well and especially the oppression exerted by language that had the power to supersede the individual with webs of predetermined meanings. Artaud revolted against "other"-ness at the everyday experiential level. He wanted to have done with representation and its implicit judgments and to experience a radical self-presence in the immediate moment. "Cruelty" for his ideal actor implied the rejection of all familiar codes through which the self functions socially. And he saw in theatre the chance to free oneself from these codes and live intensely in the "now" in a way no different from the lived self-presence. Derrida summarizes the paradox this way: "Artaud kept himself as close as possible to the limit: the possibility and impossibility of pure theatre. Presence, in order to be presence and self-presence, has always already begun to represent itself, has always already been penetrated" (1978, 249). Artaud's experience of the simulated city of the Exposition suggests that the limit of his impossible metaphysical event might lie in a similarly impossible geography. Jonas Barish adds that Artaud's city would be populated by an equally impossible anthropology: "The theatre seems to be committing itself to a science-fiction-like attempt to re-invent the human, as if we were all suddenly to wake up on a new planet, and had to recommence the history of the race anew, with no reference to the past other than that of repudiation" (1981, 459).

In *Ephemeral Vistas* Paul Greenhalgh calls the 1931 Paris Exposition "the most spectacular of French imperial displays since 1900" (1988, 69). This grandeur confronted visitors the moment they entered the Bois de Vincennes fairgrounds. At the main entrance, towers inscribed with the names of explorers and colonizers flanked an illuminated fountain. Beyond this, two monumental buildings, Scylla-and-Charybdis-like, flanked the way to the rest of the park: to the North, the permanent Musée des Colonies (the only building not torn down after the Exposition) and to the South, the Cité Internationale des Informations. Lyautey conceived the Cité des Informations as a building in which the whole extent of the Exposition "might be summarized for the benefit of the hurried visitor" (quoted in "English Week in Paris" 1931, 13). The building served as a nucleus. It was a site for "over 100 congresses, at which men of all nationalities discussed some particular aspect of Colonial administration" (*Times* 1931a, 11). With its counterpart building, the Musée, it served as part of a complex set of portals to the world of the Exposition. Just beyond these two buildings was the Porte de Picpus, after which the fairgrounds spread throughout the forest in a confusion of disparate vendors, displays, native artifacts, simulacra, and peoples. Portals run strongly through Artaud's early writing as signs through which invisible forces cross into the world. Passing through these gateways with their columns and monuments to explorers and colonizers, he may have felt a transformative crossing.

The disparate nature of the fairgrounds required a unifying aesthetic, as a reviewer for *The New Statesman* observed: "Styles mingle so admirably together. There is an aesthetic proper to exhibitions, a sort of evening party aesthetic" (Birrell 1931, 78). This "aesthetic" replaced the specific locales of the cultures represented. At night, when the Balinese troupe performed, the aesthetic became surrealistic as electric spotlights illuminated simulated temples and romantic fountains, creating a spectacular display of light and shadow amid the forest of Vincennes. The spectators who came to see the Balinese dancers had to travel from the Western gates past a landscape of fragments, possibly to be ferried across a lake of many fountains and illuminated mists, before reaching the Dutch pavilion.

The Exposition contained approximately twenty-five pavilions, two-thirds of them French and the rest Portuguese, Belgian, Italian, Brazilian, Danish, American, and Dutch. The pavilions ranged from reproduced African villages to a monumental reproduction of the Khmer temple of Angkor-Vat, commonly praised as the Exposition's most impressive spectacle. Illuminated at night, it inspired this description: "This vast and most monstrous edifice, palace and cathedral combined, raises its twisted cupolas to an electric heaven in solemn and awful majesty. Nothing could be more superbly arranged than the projectors that force out its colour, and reflect again in the surrounding moats the infinite labour of its sculpture" (Birrell 1931, 78). All the buildings were reproduced in an architectural style evocative of the respective countries, yet they were also designed to catch visitors' attention. Louis Harl comments in *Commonweal* on how the spectacles overflowed their pavilions, dispersing "native culture" in overlapping waves through the grounds: "Hundreds of natives of every race and climate have been brought to Paris for the show. . . . Only native boats ply the waters of the lake, and native food is cooked in the restaurants by the natives" (1931, 236). In keeping with Lyautey's project, a consistent style of layout and lighting and signs served to contain all this diversity, a fact much appreciated by the *Times* correspondent, employing a light/dark imagery in a racist metaphor in praise of colonial grace: "They could truly claim to have brought light into dark places and given life to doomed peoples" (*Times* 1931b, 11). The Exposition inevitably facilitated Artaud's interpretation—and misunderstanding. He would easily have accepted this "cafe atmosphere." He wrote admiringly of carnivals and earlier that year had praised a set of cafes he visited in Berlin that reproduced foreign surroundings through cunning stagecraft (Artaud 1976, 177). He surely would have misunderstood this brilliant spectacle as a power beyond Western reason, rays pushing out from a terrible Buddha for destruction and salvation. Perhaps he glimpsed in the spectacle an implicit subversion of the colonial project to which the colonial authorities themselves were blind.

Artaud also misunderstood the aims of the Dutch and the Balinese, whose joint presentation at the Exposition emerged from an already modern colonial effort at cultural redefinition. During the 1920s Balinese and Dutch cultural leaders together popularized and commercialized a form of dance-drama that soon became persuasive to tourists and Balinese alike. This gamelan with dancers of the village of Peliatan was the first Balinese ensemble to perform in Europe. Paris removed the dance-drama from its connection to the religiously oriented geography of Bali itself. On Bali all space is organized for religious purposes according to the axis from the most holy mountain, Gunung Agung, to the ocean. In a sense the Paris Exposition performed the ultimate subversion of Balinese cosmography and history for the sake of commerce and Western aesthetics. Nevertheless, Sukawati and his troupe participated with the Dutch and added the international tour to Balinese performance conventions.

The Dutch constructed their pavilion in the northeastern corner of the fairgrounds. They situated Balinese culture at the center of their display, celebrating the protected status the island had acquired as the non-Muslim jewel of the Dutch colonies. In consultation with Walter Spies, an influential German expatriate painter living in Bali, Dutch architect Pieter Moojen constructed a pavilion that combined elements of several Indonesian architectural traditions but focused on replication of Balinese space and suggestions of Hindu and Buddhist heritage.[1] The "principal pavilion" combined Javanese, Sumatran, and Balinese architectural styles and sported a *barong* mask above an entrance copied from Balinese temples. The entrance chamber juxtaposed a frieze detailing the "history" of Dutch colonialism to dioramas of traditional Javanese and Balinese village life and to display cases of native artifacts. Statues included a "Buddha" and "bodhisattva." Thus, spectators entering the pavilion confronted at once signs of colonialism, native culture, and the Hindu-Buddhist tradition.

Artaud, however, visiting the Exposition in August, would have seen a far less elaborate version of this original pavilion. On 28 June the principal pavilion burned down almost completely, and only the temple reproductions and grounds were left. Holland scrambled to reassemble a proper "representation," but most of the artifacts had perished. Moojen built a considerably less-impressive edifice in five weeks' time (*L'Il-lustration* 1931, 575), which means that it neared completion when Artaud arrived. He would have passed through this revised pavilion to reach the performance space.

The Balinese theatre, situated in an enclosed courtyard adjacent to the pavilion, replicated a Balinese temple, copied "in scrupulous detail" down to little "offering niches" ("Album" 1931, n.p.). The choice to replicate a temple for the performance suggests a desire on the part of the KPM (the Dutch tourist organization that administered Bali) and perhaps Walter Spies to frame the performance in a ritual context. The Balinese performers, however, understood it as a commercial venture. They performed none of the most sacred dances, used unconsecrated masks, and greatly abbreviated the forms. Furthermore, according to Robert Rickner, the space and staging techniques were already highly Western: "This program was given a roofed proscenium-stage theatre, with atmosphere provided by the techniques of Western stage lighting, and with a clear-cut division between the audience seated in the auditorium and the actors and musicians on stage" (1972, 38–39). This reflected a growing pattern of merging Balinese architecture with Western theatrical configurations that now pervades Balinese stages, as in

---

[1] I have not found sufficient evidence to differentiate clearly how authority was negotiated between Walter Spies, Moojen, the KPM, and the Dutch government. I have found no specific references to Bobbie Bruyns, the KPM's chief administrator on Bali, as playing any role in the organization of the pavilion, but as he was the KPM's agent and Spies's personal friend, it seems likely that he was involved.

the case of the hybrid architecture of the Pusat Seni Denpasar that houses the annual Bali Arts Festival. Nevertheless, European audiences were led to believe that they were seeing genuine ritual performances. In a Parisian interview Cokorda Raka Sukawati, the leader of the troupe, claimed: "These are almost always sacred dances. To thank Buddha for having made us what we are, we can never dance too much" (Interview 1931). Sukawati was a shrewd *ksatriya* (member of the ruling class) who had first encountered Walter Spies in his own palace in 1925, a contact that helped Sukawati turn the Ubud and Peliatan area into Bali's center for cultural tourism. In 1931 he clearly desired to popularize the representation of an ancient Balinese ritual culture with Hindu-Buddhist roots while simultaneously tailoring the commercial program to avoid sacrilege. We can only speculate on whether this produced controversy in religious or cultural circles in Bali, but it seems likely that some Balinese leaders would have had strong reservations about the display.

This first "full gamelan with dancers" consisted of about thirty musicians and twenty dancers ("Album" 1931; see also Prunieres 1931, 8:8). Alongside Sukawati (the highest ranking *ksatriya* figure in the Ubud region), Anak Agung Mandera (Ubud's second highest *ksatriya* and headman of Peliatan) led the troupe. The dance troupe must have also contained at least six prepubescent girls to dance the *legong*, at least one young man for the *baris* and *kebyar*, and two dancers for a *barong*. Sukawati was a bold, energetic, and ingenious man—so much so that he acquired a Parisian wife despite the Dutch authorities' severe restrictions to the movements of members of the troupe.[2] In this extraordinary circumstance he and Mandera (who most likely led his own village gamelan) may have functioned like Western directors.

Leonard Pronko quotes the entire program of the Balinese concert, yet this information leaves tantalizing uncertainties (1967, 24–27). It lists names of dances that equivocally relate to known dances, such as the *gong* dance and the *rakshaka*, but it also seems to double some performances. The story of King Lasem occurs twice in a row, and an Arjuna episode from the *Mahabharata* may have been performed three times. Such narrative and character repetitions may have reenforced the

---

[2]According to accounts by Anak Agung Mandera (quoted in Coast 1958, 58) and Prunieres (1931), the Dutch attempted to keep the Balinese contained within the hotel when they were not performing and even made them pay their own living expenses, paying them no salary. Sukawati returned to Paris in 1932 to bring his wife back to Bali (Sukawati 1979, 18).

audiences' reading of elements as archetypal and perhaps inspired Artaud to develop his concepts of "hieroglyphic acting" and the "double."

The program resembles nothing so much as the tourist samplers that had already begun to evolve on the island itself. Balinese cultural authorities distinguished these from the genuine and potent ritual performances. The dance-dramas performed in Paris were unconsecrated, heavily abridged, and for the most part modern in form. In a single performance, which ran from 9:30 to 11:00, the troupe performed a *kebyar duduk*, a *janger*, a *legong*, a *baris*, and a *barong* dance-drama, interconnected by gamelan interludes. Many of these forms could last several hours in a nontouristic context. The Parisian audiences were allowed to experience a sampling within the span of an hour and a half. The *kebyar*, the *janger*, and the modern *baris* were all under fifty years old. In fact, the *kebyar duduk* was only first performed in 1925 by the first Balinese celebrity dancer, I Nyoman Mario, so this piece must have been performed either by its originator himself (of which there is no record) or by an early disciple. The gamelan itself seems to have been a modern *gong kebyar* rather than one of several older gamelan configurations. Inasmuch as even the *legong* (originally a court form) and the *barong* (which evolved from pre-Hindu animistic rituals) were presented in acceptably secular revised forms, the entire program failed to predate the Dutch colonization. Nevertheless, it was described as fully representative of ancient Balinese Hindu-Buddhist culture. Furthermore, the extreme brevity of the samples must have necessitated as severe an adaptation of the performance in time as the new stage configuration did in space. A performance supposedly representative of Balinese culture was crammed into a quick, easily digestible showcase. These "ancient timeless dance-dramas" were really either recent forms or secular restagings of sacred forms, all done in an ersatz temple that was by necessity outside the cosmological orientation a temple would have had on the island of Bali proper. The Colonial Exposition, in short, snatched Balinese performance out of its context and adapted and revised it so severely that it was no longer genuine in any sense. And yet, ironically, it may have come as close as any real event could to catching Artaud's vision of an immediate, self-consuming theatre piece.

In the last days of the Exposition, *Commonweal* commentator Padraic Colum wrote about the "City-to-be-forsaken": "A band plays beside the column that stands for, I suppose, the glories of French colonial enterprise, ending all this, and in one of the buildings speeches are being made declaring that the French people have been made conscious of how far-flung and magnificent their colonial domain actually is. And I walk down a street that is bordered with African carvings—warriors and sorcerers—all solemn, burthened and unrelievable, and feel that the forest with its terrors is not far distant" (1932, 662). In this ephemeral city-forest, Artaud, Lyautey, the KPM, and Sukawati converged in a matrix of misunderstandings. They set about reframing various modernities. As the West modernized the East, the East also modernized the West, in each case mingling traditions with a distinct modernity. As in all colonialist and primitivist interactions, each side redefines the other. Imagining an impossible self through his misunderstanding, Artaud exclaimed: "After an instant the magic identification is made: WE KNOW IT IS WE WHO WERE SPEAKING" (1958, 67).

Works Cited

"Album de L'Exposition Colonial de Paris, 1931." 1931. In *L'Exposition,* special edition.

Artaud, Antonin. [1930] 1976. "Letter to René Allendy" [12 July]. In *Antonin Artaud: Selected Writings,* ed. Susan Sonntag, trans. Helen Weaver. Berkeley: University of California Press.

———. 1958. "On the Balinese Theatre." In *The Theatre and Its Double,* trans. Mary Richards. New York: Grove Wiendenfeld.

Bandem, I Made, and Fredrik Eugene deBoer. 1995. *Balinese Dance in Transition.* Kuala Lumpur: Oxford University Press.

Barish, Jonas. 1981. *The Anti-theatrical Prejudice.* Berkeley: University of California Press.

Bharucha, Rustom. 1990. *Theatre and the World.* London: Routledge.

Birrell, Francis. 1931. "Thought on the French Colonial Exposition." In *The New Statesman and Nation.* Vol. 2, 18 July.

Coast, John. 1958. *Dancing Out of Bali.* London: Faber and Faber.

Colum, Padraic. 1932. "The City-to-Be-Forsaken." *Commonweal,* 8 April.

Comaroff, Jean, and John Comaroff, eds. 1993. *Modernity and Its Malcontents.* Chicago: University of Chicago Press.

Derrida, Jacques. 1978. "The Theatre of Cruelty and the Closure of Representation." In *Writing and Difference,* trans. Alan Bass. Chicago: University of Chicago Press.

"English Week in Paris." 1931. *Times* (London), 23 July.

Greenhalgh, Paul. 1988. *Ephemeral Vistas.* Manchester: Manchester University Press.

Harl, Louis P. 1931. "The Exposition at Paris." *Commonweal,* 1 July.

"Holland Salvages Relics." 1931. *New York Times,* 30 June.

L'Illustration (Paris). 1931. No. 4616.

Innes, Christopher. 1993. *Avant-Garde Theatre, 1892–1992.* London: Routledge.

Interview with Cokorda Raka Sukawati. 1931. *Paris-Soir,* 25 June.

Lyautey, Marshal. 1931. "France and the International Colonial Exposition." In *Nineteenth Century and After*. Vol. 109.

Pronko, Leonard. 1967. *Theatre East and West*. Berkeley: University of California Press.

Prunieres, Henry. 1931. "Native Balinese Music in Paris." *New York Times*, 27 September.

Rickner, Robert. 1972. Theatre as Ritual: Artaud's Theatre of Cruelty and the Balinese Barong. Ph.D. diss., University of Hawaii.

Sukawati, Tjokorda Gede Agung. 1979. *Reminiscences of a Balinese Prince*. Dictated to Rosemary Hilbery. Honolulu: University of Hawaii Press.

Times. 1931a. "Marshal Lyautey's Achievement." 16 November.

Times. 1931b. 7 May.

Turner, Victor. 1982. *From Ritual to Theatre*. New York: Performing Arts Journal Press.

Theatre at the Crossroads

Eastern and Western Influences
on a Nepali Street Theatre Production

Carol Davis

*F*ROM MY JOURNAL, 12 April 1996:

This steep ascent feels never-ending: we climb up and up, still up and ever up. It is hot, it is humid, I am exhausted, I am out of breath, sweat is soaking back and pack. We pass *chortens,* pass *chautaaras,* pass terraced rice fields too steeply stacked—how can anyone work on them, how can anyone eke out an existence in this steep, thirsty, dusty terrain? Eventually we pass people on the trail, we pass glances and glares, pass questioning looks and suspicious stares. Finally we arrive at this little village, so small, so parched: a fetid lake in the baking sun, no shops, only scattered mud-brick homes and a school, a small mud-floored school with a corrugated tin roof that bakes the students when it's hot, freezes them when cold. After a performance at dawn in the large village below, we climbed 2000 feet virtually straight up in three and a half hours to reach Arupokari, and we collapse, sprawled in the shade of a clump of bamboo, to find refreshment in the breath of a breeze. Ridge upon ridge of high terraced mountains stretch before me and all around me. In the last hour of daylight we perform our play for the residents of Arupokari just back from their fields; 500 people crowd around us in the schoolyard, eager and intent, they watch and listen to all we can give: they hungrily consume our play.

The play performed that evening in Arupokari was a multicultural attempt to address the health crisis in rural Nepal. Five Nepali actors and I worked together to create the play that has now been performed for more than 30,000 villagers throughout the foothills of Nepal. Our production, *Hamro Swastia Hamro Hatmachaa* (Our Health Is in Our Hands), reflects the theatrical and cultural heritage of the artists involved in its creation and development. It is a performance piece in which the crosscurrents of Eastern and Western drama are manifest, and it functions to benefit an information-bereft population.

Sandwiched between the major Eastern powers of China and India, and located in the unforgiving terrain of the Himalayas, Nepal is one of the most rugged countries in the world as well as one of the poorest. Approximately 90 percent of Nepal's population of nineteen million live in rural villages, many of which are completely inaccessible by roads or by air and most of which lack electricity and sanitary drinking water. The combination of Nepal's adverse geography and its extreme poverty results in health and hygienic conditions that rank among the most substandard in the world. Nepal's infant, early childhood, and maternal mortality rates are among the highest in the world, and life expectancy is minimal after the age of fifty for men, and forty-three for women.

Building community awareness about health and sanitation is a key requisite for changing unsanitary behavior, preventing disease, and ultimately ensuring longer, healthier lives. The lack of electricity in remote areas prohibits the use of educational video and radio programs, and rural illiteracy impedes education through brochures and books. Consequently, live, mobile, and free street theatre provides the perfect medium to educate the greatest number of people in a nonthreatening and easily comprehensible way. Actors who travel by foot, carry backpacks of costumes and props, and climb sheer mountain trails to reach remote villages can penetrate where more modern, hi-tech forms of communication do not reach.

In order to ascertain the most threatening diseases and discern the most readily accessible means for the Nepalis to avoid or remedy them, I conducted research with Nepali and American health professionals. With research results in hand, I located actors, and together we evolved our informative comic drama. In our effort to communicate and entertain effectively, we drew on our respective theatrical ancestries and created a piece unique in Nepali production.

The actors and I then traveled first by bus and truck to road's end and then by foot to reach remote Himalayan villages at great distances from even the most rudimentary health clinics. We performed our play in schools, village centers, and at crossroads along the trail, for children and adults, reaching at least some of the neglected rural population who would otherwise miss out on essential information. We were always greeted with curiosity and often with suspicion. At times we were suspected of being nongovernment Communist terrorists because politically motivated vendettas had occurred in the areas we were touring. Conversely, we were also taken for government spies. However, once we gathered audiences onto the natural amphitheatre of a hillside, or into a simple circle on the ground, we set them at ease with our style, at once familiar and foreign, educational and entertaining.

Unlike its southern and northern neighbors, India and China, Nepal does not have an elaborate tradition of formal or folk theatre. Dance representations of religious figures take place at specific times of year, at festivals associated with certain deities, yet traditions such as India's *Jatra, Nautanki,* and *Tamasha* have not moved north into Nepal. Certain techniques used in the *Veethi nataka* of India, however, were also employed for our *saadak natak* (street-drama), *Hamro Swastia Hamro Hatmachaa.*

In Nepal's major cities modern *saadak natak* has just begun to offer a vital source of historical, educational, and cultural information. The recent prodemocracy movement, for example, was fueled, supported, broadcast, and mythologized by activists who found street theatre more effective than making speeches. Theatre has provided Nepali artist/activists with an unrivaled means to teach social awareness.

In rural Nepal, dance and drama are occasionally used to teach religious concepts and cultural history; for example, in the shadow of Mt. Everest, Buddhist monks of the mountain-dwelling Sherpa culture perform dance-dramas that have roots in Tibetan ritual. These dramas prove to be instructive agents and communal building blocks. For the most part rural audiences have never seen film or television, and their keen interest in the religious dramas attests to their hunger for the stories, images, and enchantment live theatre offers.

Before rehearsals began for *Hamro Swastia Hamro Hatmachaa,* I observed the work of the foremost Nepali street-theatre company, Sarwanam, as its founding director and playwright, Asesh Malla (a professor at Tribhuvan University and a member of the Royal Academy) rehearsed the actors. Malla spoke the lines of dialogue to them and had them memorize the words as he blocked each scene. Although Malla's plays may not be written down at the time of initial rehearsals, they are in no way improvised. Malla conceives, directs, and writes the plays and dictates all manner of stage business and dialogue to his actors. His style results in plays that explain situations without necessarily dramatizing them; he uses scant characterization and his serious plays "delight" not through laughter or spectacle but primarily through the audience's identification with problems and situations. Malla's actors have little to no experience with the personally creative rehearsal and character-building process that we in the West cultivate and value. As with many Eastern theatre forms, transmission occurs through a process of direct imitation and repetition.

The Eastern heritage of *Hamro Swastia Hamro Hatmachaa* is

reflected, then, not in the rehearsal process but in the use of characters familiar to the Nepali audiences and with whom they can readily identify, even with only minimal distinguishing costumes or props. Familiar characters evince traditional roles and role playing: Brahmans are in positions of authority; women farm, tend livestock and children, and cook for school goings-ons; other women, weak from malnutrition, die in childbirth. Musical instruments and song elements from Nepali folk tradition find their way into this performance and function in part to attract what could be reluctant audiences. Clearly the Nepali actors further influenced the production by incorporating a devotional aspect into our educational and entertaining theatre piece.

My participation in *Hamro Swastia Hamro Hatmachaa* as a Western theatre artist is evident in the concepts and techniques I brought to the production. The Horatian idea that the function of theatre is "to delight and instruct" is apparent in the very basis and conception of the entire project. My background in Western theatre history made inevitable the transmission of concepts found in certain theatre practices such as Brecht's *Lehrstücke* or the agitprop theatres of revolutionary Russia and of America in the 1930s and 1960s. Western *dianoia* subtly infuses the play with the humanist suggestion that potential for well-being rests in the hands of the individual more than in the hands of God, hence the title of our play, *Our Health Is in Our Hands*. The Hindu actors had to become comfortable with this idea before we could begin rehearsing. The legacy of Western theatre also appears in techniques derived from *commedia dell'arte* and the physical theatre of Molière, from El Teatro Campesino and the San Francisco Mime Troupe. Rehearsal techniques and expectations unfamiliar to Nepali actors stretched their capabilities and resulted in performances fresh and unique.

The actors were encouraged to explore, improvise, and participate in a collectively developed production. After conducting research on the problems and viable solutions to Nepal's health crisis, the actors and I improvised ways of dramatizing our message. I let them know that if we had something to say, we would have to create our own statement as much from experience as from research. This statement, of course, could not be presented in the abstract way of the masked monks dancing in the mountains of Nepal; rather it had to be conveyed as concrete information that, if implemented, could change forever patterns of behavior that had perpetually plagued the Nepalis.

I also brought to Nepal my experience of working with Jorge Huerta and William Virchis in Teatro Magica Mascara, and I modeled our rehearsal process after that of El Teatro Campesino. In his book, *Chicano*

Theatre: Themes and Forms, Jorge Huerta describes the process used by Luis Valdez to evolve the first *actos* of El Teatro Campesino:

> With each improvisation of their daily struggles, these *campesinos* demonstrate to Valdez that there is a message to be dramatized. . . . Those that choose to get involved will become the collective authors of the Teatro's first *actos:* improvised scenes that present the realities of the struggle. Under Valdez's guidance, his group will explore the characters and situations that must be exposed in order to educate the farmworkers. There is an immediacy about the evening's improvisations. These are not actors portraying characters from a playwright's pen; they are people expressing their own experiences. (1982, 13)

We considered it essential that our audiences be familiar with certain of our characters so that they could readily empathize with them and recognize their situations. To find characters recognizable to all Nepalis was a task I had to put to the actors who knew the culture intimately. Nepal is an ethnically and religiously diverse country, and although approximately 75 percent of Nepalis are Hindu, they represent more than twenty-five distinct ethnic groups. Nepal is also approximately 20 percent Buddhist. We eventually settled on the character of Yamraj, lord of the dead and god of heaven (Yamalok). This deity is variously represented as Yama in Hinduism and as Yamantaka in Tibetan Buddhism, so we could be sure that the majority of our audiences would have at least a limited familiarity with Yamraj, and because his horned crown identifies him to all who are familiar with the Hindu/Buddhist pantheon, his costuming was quickly suggested. The second character we determined to use is an archetype of the wise village elder. It was important to us to support traditional ways of healing and problem solving. We wanted to integrate our information into the existing structure of Nepali village life, and we did this by promoting respect for the knowledge of the elders. To this end we determined to use the figure of Gangaram, an elder with wisdom and compassion widely known in folktale and legend.

These characters, Yamraj from Yamalok (heaven) and Gangaram from Prithvi (earth), were the key to organizing the structure of our play. Yamraj is concerned with the overcrowding of heaven by the dead who come from Nepal. He looks down on earth to discover the cause of the mass exodus. He sees that the water sources are polluted by human waste and excrement, that children are dying from diarrheal dehydration and preventable diseases, that people do not practice good personal hygiene or take appropriate action for fevers and infections, and perhaps most important, that some women are treated almost as servants in their own homes and are not nourished properly when they are pregnant, so that they die in childbirth along with their stillborn babies.

By alternating between Yamraj and his assistant Yamdoot in Yamalok, and Gangaram and mortals on Prithvi, we created a decidedly non-Western episodic structure. Our play, plotless and barely linear, became epic storytelling. We juxtaposed Yamalok and Prithvi and moved from heaven to earth with no more to transport us than the music of the *basuri,* the slender and simple bamboo flute found throughout Nepal. Village characters would engage in various scenes. One of them involves a dispute about the relative merits of building a latrine and about its location: should it be built on the banks of a river so the effluence may be washed away with the rain, or should it be located far from the water source to keep the water clean for those who live downstream and use it for bathing and cooking? Gangaram sets the villagers straight and even shows them a chart of a latrine properly made from stone and a little lumber. Suddenly we are transported again to Yamalok; this happens with the crashing of *chellig* (small strong bronze cymbals), the beating of the *maadol* (the drum like a small Indian *tabla*), and the twirling of colored fabrics spun by the actresses in a whirling frenzied dance of color.

The dramatic creation of Yamraj and Gangaram was easier for the Nepali actors to understand than was the theatrical personification of these very different characters. In the *legong* of Bali the young dancers seem to make no differentiation between the character types they portray, and it is impossible for the uninitiated observer to differentiate between the king of Lasan and the princess he courts. Just so, in initial rehearsals of our play, it was impossible for me to distinguish between one character and another, between God and mortal. Although Yamraj needed to be fearsome and larger than life, the actor portraying him initially played Yamraj exactly as he played the mortal who didn't want a latrine built upriver from his home.

Thus, we entered a phase of rehearsal focused on characterization. We worked to distinguish Yamraj from his assistant Yamdoot. As we did this it became clear to me that Yamdoot would be responsible for the comic aspects of the scenes in Yamalok. By juxtaposing a huge, fierce, authoritarian commander with a small, spry, and fawning assistant, we could draw in the audience with humor and hold their attention so that they would receive our important information. For the scenes down on earth, we clearly needed characters such as that scoundrel Scapin. But these actors had no experience with physical theatre, with slapstick, or with the *lazzi* I knew we would employ to enchant the children. Nepali theatre traditions had not familiarized them with physical theatre, with the pratfalls of *commedia,* or even with the obvious antics of the Three Stooges. I taught the actors to do somersaults, to duck as scene partners swept boards over their heads, to take a pratfall, and then pull their partners down with them when they try to give them a hand up. I encouraged them to use the shape and size and motion of their bodies in space to communicate beyond what the words would do.

We in the West take for granted the world of physical comedy. We grow up with Saturday morning cartoons, with Buster Keaton and Charlie Chaplin. Our training of actors using mask work, effort/shape, gymnastics, and dance was altogether foreign to these actors. Once they understood, however, that onstage they had freedom to unleash the energy of their bodies, they grew inestimably in their physicalizations so that in performance, Yamdoot spends as much time leaping into the air as he does with his feet on the ground.

Given similar freedom in determining the dialogue, the actors explored the use of puns, topical allusions, mimicry, jokes, and songs in ways they had never before experienced. I told them about the traditions of *commedia dell'arte* and the way the actors would establish a scenario and then improvise the dialogue. They responded enthusiastically to this artistic license. Our first performance was unlike any of our rehearsals, for when we began to tell our stories the actors came alive; they spoke dialogue they had never even considered before. The magic of performing and communicating was alive in them and it opened a wellspring of creative and exciting expression. Each performance was better than the last, and the actors continued to build on what they discovered. The act of performing became for them the creative act of composing so that we were able to develop new scenes as we traveled and as we responded to our audiences.

One other decidedly Eastern feature of our performance was that the actors would not begin the play without acknowledging Narteswari, a feminine/masculine aspect of Shiva, the patron and god of music, the dance, and drama. To make this ritual offering of interest to our audiences, we performed it as a song. We sang of our stage, the earth, of our light, the sun, of ourselves the actors and our audience as members of the same family, and of the larger village community that is the globe, and we sang, *"Jaya, Jaya, Jaya, Hey Narteswari."* This was the least theatrical portion of our show; we quickly followed it with another song, and with that we broke from Nepali tradition. We did not insulate ourselves from the audience. We made eye contact as we sang, much to the discomfort and delight of our audience members. I would catch the eye of a young child sitting in the dust at my feet and motion washing my hands as I sang, *"Hat dhune bane basalone"* (roughly translated that's "Let's all wash our hands") or "*Rog lai tada bhagavan*" ("Let's wash off the dirt of field and toilet"). We sang of these things, and on each line I would catch the eyes of a different child. Usually the child would squeal with delight, that this strange, blond being in this crude but magical circle of a stage would single him out and welcome him to the world of theatre. When I sang, "*Jaya, Jaya, Jaya, Hey Narteswari,*" I would make eye contact with a woman and so link both of us to the goddess's name.

In the last scene of our play, in Yamalok, a woman enters. She had died in childbirth because, after feeding her husband's family, there was never enough food for herself. Yamraj charges the village audience to take care of their women, to remember that pregnant women need enough food for two, that they need nourishment to produce healthy babies, and that healthy babies can better fight disease and live longer. At one performance a Nepali friend sat in the audience next to some village women, some mothers, and when this scene was over, our friend heard a woman say, "This is our story."

In my altruistic drive to do the right thing, did I unconscionably alter forever Nepali folk theatre? Was it cultural imperialism that fused the currents of Eastern and Western drama to prompt a tear from these hardy souls seated in the midday sun, the monsoon rain, the dawn preceding work, or the dusk following it? I used and honored certain Eastern traditions in this production, but, yes, I imposed Western traditions as well. In doing so I forged a link in the chain of world theatre's evolution, and I must accept responsibility for the repercussions of this cross-cultural exchange that may resonate forever in Nepal. However, I also was changed by the process and brought back to the West experience, knowledge, and a special gift from the East.

Each time the actors entered our performance area, the space we created merely by seating children and adults on the ground in a circle around us, they reached down and touched the earth and then put their fingers to their foreheads, mindful always that this work we do, this piece of fun, this bit of entertaining education, is our offering to humanity and to the spirits that nourish actor and audience alike. These days, every time I enter a studio or a theatre to rehearse or to perform, I too touch the ground that is our working space, our stage, and then I reach up and touch my head.

Work Cited

Huerta, Jorge. 1982. *Chicano Theatre: Themes and Forms.* Tempe, Ariz.: Bilingual Press.

Dancing on Shifting Ground

The Balinese *Kecak*
in Cross-Cultural Perspective

Claudia Orenstein

*T*HE EVER GROWING NUMBER of tourists who flock to the small island of Bali expecting to soak up both sun and Balinese culture may, when watching the island's bountiful offerings of tourist performances, mistakenly assume that they are getting a glimpse into the ancient performance traditions of a primitive culture. This feeling is perhaps most keenly felt by tourists watching the popular *kecak,* or "monkey dance." In the *kecak* a large chorus of bare-chested men sit close together in a circle and vocalize a complex rhythmic chant. They accompany their human orchestra with group movements, sometimes quickly fluttering their fingers with outstretched arms, sometimes moving their shoulders back and forth, hands on waists, in pulsating, isolated, staccato gestures as they turn their heads from side to side. What audiences are seeing, however, is a performance that is as much the product of a cross-cultural interaction of East and West as it is an artifact of Balinese culture. Tracing the cross-cultural influences that have shaped the *kecak* dance can shed light on broader issues, for it illustrates the complex patterns of interaction inherent in any creative process involving intersecting, diverse cultures.

The *kecak* dance is often called the "monkey dance" because the percussive chanting that accompanies the performance sounds like the chattering of monkeys. The name also derives from the monkey king Hanuman's army of monkeys who help Rama track down and recapture his abducted wife Sita in the Hindu *Ramayana* epic. The sound has been compared as well to the croaking of frogs. Moreover, it is believed to be a vocal imitation of, or at least an alternative to, the gamelan orchestra that accompanies almost all other Balinese dance performances. The *cak* chorus on its own is found as an accompaniment to an older group of dances or exorcist rites known as *Sang Hyang,* performances "characterized by spirit possession" (Bandem and deBoer 1995, 151). Among these traditions are the *Sang Hyang Dedari,* in which young girls become possessed by the spirits of celestial nymphs, and the *Sang Hyang Jaran,* in which male performers are possessed by a horse spirit. In these ritual dances, the complex "cak, cak, cak" rhythms of the chorus create and maintain the trance of dancers (de Zoete and Spies 1973, 67–85). Although the *kecak* dance does not involve spirit possession, it does combine a large male *cak* chorus with dancers who act out episodes from the *Ramayana.*

The *kecak,* therefore, combines aspects of an indigenous tribal rite with a Hindu story that has passed to Bali from India through Java. The combination of these two elements, tribal chant and Hindu tale, owes a great deal to the artist, dancer, musician Walter Spies, who was himself something of a cultural hybrid. Born in Russia of German parents (one of half Scottish background), Spies spent his formative years in Moscow and Dresden, a period of internment during World War I with tribal groups in the Ural mountains, some time in Berlin, some in Holland, and some in Yogyakarta, and the last fifteen of his forty-seven years in Bali. Spies definitely contributed to shaping the *kecak* dance into its present form, but sorting out the exact extent of his contribution is difficult. According to Hans Rhodius, Spies reworked the *kecak* during the 1931 filming of *The Island of Demons,* directed by Victor Baron von Plessen and his collaborator Dr. Dahlsheim. For this movie, Rhodius says, Spies "remodeled" the *kecak:* "He increased the number of participants to more than a hundred young men sitting in a circle, and also introduced the figure of the dancer-narrator who recited, in the light of a central standing lamp, tales from the *Ramayana* involving the exploits of Hanoman, the monkey-general" (Rhodius and Darling 1980, 37). The original *kecak* referred to here, reworked for the film, seems to be the traditional *cak* chorus. Spies is credited with enlarging that chorus and adding a telling of the *Ramayana.* According to Rhodius, Spies's reputation as an expert on Bali and on all things Balinese meant that his participation in the film would guarantee the authenticity of the film's story, setting, and dances—this despite his liberal "remodeling" of traditional forms.

Philip F. McKean, however, attributes the creation of what he calls the "tourist *ketjak*" to a Balinese, Ida Bagus Mudiara, from Bona village in Gianyar province. According to McKean, Mudiara was asked in 1930 by the royal house of Gianyar to "prepare an orchestra for ceremonies": "He began to blend the *suara gamelan* ('voice' *gamelan*) of *ketjak* with the epic Hindu poem, the *Ramayana,* which was at that time enacted through *wayang wong* (human actors acting legendary parts). . . . According to Mudiara he decided to substitute the voices of the *ketjak* chorus for the *gamelan* using the chorus as actors in the story as it seemed appropriate, and then selecting portions of the *Ramayana* for performance" (McKean 1979, 299). McKean states that it was not until 1932 that Spies saw this version of the *kecak* and then "commissioned performances for tourists" (299). These tourist performances then led to a shortened version of the dance that told only a portion of the epic tale.

Michel Picard, however, tells yet a third version of the story. His version comes from another Balinese, I Limbak from Bedulu. Picard says of Limbak that "at the end of the 1920s he started incorporating *baris* movements into the role of the *cak* leader. Walter Spies liked this innovation and suggested that he should devise a spectacle based on the *Ramayana,* accompanied solely by the *cak* chorus in lieu of the usual *gamelan*" (Picard 1990, 60). It was apparently from this base that Spies then "reworked the *kecak* to increase its dramatic impact" (60).

Spies's own writings somewhat corroborate Picard's version. In *Dance and Drama in Bali* Spies and his collaborator, Beryl de Zoete, write of Limbak, who in their estimation should be credited with "the development of the most famous group of *ketjak,* that of north Bedoeloe." While praising I Limbak, Spies and de Zoete do suggest, in very guarded terms, that outside influence helped shape the *kecak:* "It is true that the creative effort which produced the astonishing ensemble we have attempted to describe was partly inspired by certain Europeans who felt that Limbak's great gifts as a dancer had not found their full expression in *Baris,* and urged him to make something splendid out of the *Ketjak* group of his own village. But the *Ketjak* was of purely Balinese inspiration; there were already two *Ketjak* groups in the wards of north and south Bedoeloe and there was a moment when south Bedoeloe had very much the ascendancy. What south Bedoeloe and the other well known *Ketjaks* of Bona now lack is precisely the superb unity and sense of form which Limbak has supplied" (de Zoete and Spies 1973, 83).

In this account Spies and de Zoete obviously play down Spies's own involvement, to the point of simply referring to "certain Europeans." They praise I Limbak for making something special out of his village dance troupe, especially "the superb unity and sense of form" that he had cultivated in the Bedulu *kecak.* They do not necessarily attribute to him the innovations that linked the *cak* chorus with the *Ramayana* story, but they do make a special point of stressing the very Balinese origins of the performance.

It is clear that Walter Spies had some involvement in the creation of this new dance form. To what extent is uncertain. But it is also clear that the Balinese did not simply provide the materials out of which Spies constructed something new; they were actively involved in the creative process. The difficulty we encounter tracing the origins of the *kecak* derives from the strong desire on the parts of Spies, Limbak, Mudiara, and whoever else was involved that we view the *kecak* as purely Balinese. The *kecak* and its subsequent development are all the product of an intercultural push-me-pull-you, if not outright collaboration.

Since the creation of the *kecak* sometime in the 1930s, its further development came about through a mixture of Balinese and outside influences. Although McKean had asserted that over time the *Ramayana* portions of the *kecak* were shortened, Picard states that in the 1960s it expanded to "encompass the whole epic tale" (Picard 1990, 60). This expansion, he says, resulted from the influence of Balinese students with a conservatory training and a fascination for the "Ramayana Ballet." The "Ramayana Ballet," of course, has its own multicultural origins. A Javanese dance performance that tells the whole *Ramayana* story, it was originally created in Java by a Javanese prince who was the Minister of Communications and Tourism at the time (Picard 1990, 52). As the name implies, the "Ramayana Ballet" shows strong influence from Western ballet. The Ministry designed it to cater to a foreign audience who did not understand Javanese and were unacquainted with Javanese dance forms. Thus a form that had functioned as a tourist attraction on Java became the new model for a revision of a tourist performance in Bali.

Although the *kecak* never caught on as an entertainment for the Balinese themselves (despite their interest in new forms such as the *sendratari*), it has remained a great tourist draw ever since its immediate success among foreign tourists in the thirties. Tourism continues to influence its development. According to I Made Bandem and Frederik deBoer, the new expanded version of the *kecak* that Picard mentions became so popular that travel agents "threatened to stop taking tourist buses to villages refusing to adapt their plays to the newer style" (Bandem and deBoer 1995, 131). Under this pressure the new version of the *kecak* became the standard version performed throughout the island. Such intervention could very well squelch new variants or further development of the form.

The *kecak* dance has become a performance tradition primarily for tourists, producing a reciprocal cultural relationship between its Balinese performers and their foreign audiences. Balinese villages support these tourist performances, and tourist money in turn helps the Balinese support both the *kecak* and the other artistic and religious activities that they carry on for themselves. Appreciation of Balinese cultural arts by outsiders has been a valuable resource for the Balinese in more than just economic terms. As part of Indonesia Bali is subject to continuous intervention and scrutiny from the central government in Jakarta. The Indonesian government is continually looking for ways to unify the distinct cultural communities of the numerous islands that make up Indonesia. For example, the government has sought to impose Indonesian, a Malay dialect, as the national language among the speakers of over three hundred different local languages across the archipelago. As a primarily Hindu culture within a predominantly Muslim country, Bali runs the risk of cultural absorption and repression. Avid outside interest in Balinese culture, especially its performance traditions, has helped the Balinese to preserve much of their cultural heritage. Other Indonesian communities have not been so lucky, as events in East Timor and Irian Jaya attest.

Ironically, the Indonesian government supports the development of the Balinese arts both to sustain its relationship with the West and to promote its own sense of Indonesian national identity. In 1991 the STSI (Sekolah Tinggi Seni Indonesia), the College of the Arts in Denpasar, Bali, was called upon to create performances for two occasions: the fortieth anniversary celebration of the Pacific Asia Travel Association (PATA)—an event with an international emphasis—and a celebration of the Harkitnas (Day of National Resurgence)—an event with an Indonesian national focus. Brett Hough analyzes both events and concludes that for the international PATA performance STSI could emphasize distinctly Balinese motifs more than they could for the nationally focused event. Accordingly, the STSI students and faculty created a large spectacle in the new *sendratari* style based on the conference theme, "Enrich the Environment." To highlight Balinese culture for the sake of appealing to the tourist industry, the performance included a *cak* chorus that came out in full force to greet a Garuda bird. Although the stage picture at the end of the piece showed characters representing all areas of the Indonesian archipelago, the emphasis of this event for international appeal was on Bali and Balinese performance as representative of Indonesian identity. For the national event, however, the production, again a grand spectacle, focused more on the diversity of national identities within Indonesia, toning down the Balinese cultural contributions. Nevertheless, as Hough points out, the artists in this production who performed dances from all across the archipelago were mostly Balinese (Hough 1992, 22). The Indonesian government sees Bali's ability to publicize its unique cultural identity to the outside world through its performing arts as a model for other cultural communities of Indonesia. Under Indonesia's government slogan, "unity in diversity," Bali serves as the prime example of a community that can retain its identity while at the same time representing a greater Indonesia.

The Balinese and Indonesian officials can celebrate tourism with events like these because of the enormous economic benefits they bring. However, the invasion of tourists can also mean the destruction of the very art forms that have made Bali attractive to visitors in the past. In response to this fear the Balinese have tried to cultivate two parallel sets of performance practices, one for tourists and one for the Balinese. The latter serve to maintain the sacred character of performances that take place as part of temple festivals. This situation, however, leads to some interesting dilemmas. Bandem and deBoer cite the following example (1995, 128). Because many Balinese performance traditions involve actual sacred practice, the Balinese have developed hybrid performances that cater to the needs of tourists eager to get a glimpse of these secret rites. Although these new composite dances were created in order to preserve "authentic" performance traditions from the ravages of tourism, the dancers may perform the "authentic" forms only on special occasions, whereas they perform the tourist versions regularly, sometimes several times a week. The result is often that the tourist performances become the norm for the dancers themselves, and the original performance traditions become less and less familiar.

Picard gives further examples of complications that have arisen from the well-motivated attempt to maintain some supposed "cultural purity" within Balinese performance. The distinction between sacred and profane theatrical forms, meant to support the two relatively distinct yet parallel performance traditions, seems to have little if any relevance to most Balinese. In 1967 I Gusti Gedé Raka of Saba Village, Gianyar Province, choreographed the *Panyembrama,* a new welcoming dance for greeting tourists, so that the sacred *Pendet* dance welcoming gods to the temples would not be used for this profane purpose. But eventually dancers began to perform the tourist *Panyembrama* at temple festivals. Likewise, performers who do masked *Rangda* and *Barong* dances for tourists prefer to use consecrated masks meant only for sacred temple performances. For these performers, consecrating the mask allows for the possibility of spirit possession and therefore helps both the mask and the performance to come alive. The use of consecrated objects for these supposedly "profane" daily events, however, also opens up the possibility of danger from spirit possession, requiring further precautionary ritual measures on the part of the performers.

The Balinese may not divide life into the categories of "sacred" and "profane" in the same way outsiders do. This can lead to problems in distinguishing authentic traditions of performance even when such distinction is in the service of preserving cultural heritage. The lines between authentic culture or cultural purity and hybrid or bogus culture may become easily blurred. Put into historical perspective, it is not new and innovative forms developed through contact with the outside that pose a danger to the arts of Bali. Since at least the fourteenth century, the Balinese have absorbed artistic influences from outside cultures imposed in one way or another on the island. Such a long history of cultural interaction exposes any notion of Balinese "cultural purity" as a myth. Demystifying the notion of cultural purity is no novel task but one that perhaps bears repeating in this instance.

Bali's long cross-cultural fertilization has produced a lively cultural environment in which the performing arts have flourished. The danger that lies in wait for the Balinese arts comes more from the desire to see them preserved as fixed and unchanging than from any influx of new influences. The salient distinction is not outside versus inside but fixity versus flexibility. Pressure exerted by the tourist agencies on performers to keep to one style of *kecak* is the kind of influence that leads to the deadening of the performing arts more than any other cultural pressures. What keeps performance traditions alive and popular is their ability to renew themselves continually by adapting to new situations. Even a relatively new piece, such as the *kecak* developed from international collaboration and adopted expressly for outsiders, could have a vibrant artistic life. Indeed, history shows that it has already had one. If the artists who perform it lose the freedom to modify it, however, it will itself lose its vitality. The sacred character of Balinese performance does not rule out the possibility of change. In her analysis of Yoruba ritual, anthropologist Margaret Thompson Drewal shows that, contrary to accepted views, ritual and ritual performance are not simply the static preservation and reenactment of an unchanging form (1992, xiii–xiv). In fact, what keeps both rituals and theatrical traditions alive is the interplay of abiding structure on the one hand and improvisation and innovation on the other. This kind of negotiation between custom and variation is important to the performance traditions of Bali; it can be the source of their strength rather than the herald of their demise.

The history of Bali has not been one of isolation but rather one bound up with its relationship to the outside world—Dutch colonists, European and American artists and anthropologists, Japanese occupying forces, Indonesian nationalist, communist, and democratic groups, and tourists from all over. It would be absurd to think that these powerful forces have not moved and transformed Balinese culture. The political turbulence and international conflicts that have shaped Bali in the twentieth century are not unique to this small island. What perhaps is unique to Bali is how those interactions have led so insistently to discussions of the nature of identity (what is Balinese?) and how performance has been so continually and visibly at the center of those discussions. In Bali, more than almost anywhere else, performance has become nearly synonymous with the expression of cultural identity.

The island's artistic life continues to shape and to be shaped by how others see Bali and how the Balinese see themselves. The fact that performance traditions and cultural identity are in continual flux should come as no surprise. On the contrary, what should come as a surprise is the pervasive desire of cultural observers visiting Bali to see its arts as eternal, fixed, and ahistorical. The desire to witness only the resurrection of ancient culture rites within any performance tradition implies that history is static. However, a living culture shifts and grows in response to new challenges and new influences in all areas. New cultural influences find expression through the arts both through traditional forms and through the development of new ones. How well a culture can accommodate the creative innovations of its artists is a significant measure of its own vitality. Such innovation does not require a complete break with past traditions but rather the ability of traditional forms to support new growth. The pressure to fix, delineate, or dictate Balinese performance traditions comes from a confluence of forces, including tourist agents, government policy makers, and perhaps even foreign theatre practitioners looking for the same experience that inspired Artaud, Mnouchkine, Taymore, and others. One may hope that those forces capitalizing on the popular reputation of the Balinese arts will not conspire to lead Balinese performance away from the vitality that has made it not only a tourist draw but the source of inspiration to theatre artists throughout the world.

Works Cited

Bandem, I Made, and Frederik deBoer. 1995. *Balinese Dance in Transition: Kaja and Kelod.* 2d ed. Oxford: Oxford University Press.

de Zoete, Beryl, and Walter Spies. 1973. *Dance and Drama in Bali.* Kuala Lumpur: Oxford University Press.

Drewal, Margaret Thompson. 1992. *Yoruba Ritual: Performers, Play, Agency.* Bloomington: Indiana University Press.

Hough, Brett. 1992. "Contemporary Balinese Dance Spectacles as National Ritual." Working paper #74, Monash University, Clayton, Australia.

McKean, Philip F. 1979. "From Purity to Pollution? The Balinese *Ketjak* (Monkey Dance) as Symbolic Form in Transition." In *The Imagination of Reality: Essays in Southeast Asian Coherence Systems,* ed. A. L. Becker and Aram A. Yengoyan. Norwood, N.J.: Norwood Corporation.

Picard, Michel. 1990. " 'Cultural Tourism' in Bali: Cultural Performances as Tourist Attractions." *Indonesia* 49 (April): 37–74.

Rhodius, Hans, and John Darling. 1980. *Walter Spies and Balinese Art.* Ed. John Stowell. Amsterdam: Terra Zutphen.

Robinson, Geoffrey. 1995. *The Dark Side of Paradise: Political Violence in Bali.* Ithaca: Cornell University Press.

Dancing at the Shrine of Jesus

Christianity and *Shingeki*

Kevin J. Wetmore, Jr.

Jesus and Japan: my faith is not a circle
with one center; it is an ellipse with two centers.
—Uchimura Kanzo (1925)

*T*HE STORY IS TOLD of an American bishop attending a religious congress in Japan who visited a Shinto ceremony. Afterward, he approached the Shinto priest and told him that he enjoyed the ritual, but he did not understand the theology behind it. The Shinto priest thought for a moment and then responded, "I don't think we have a theology. We just dance." This comment reveals two important concepts. First, Japanese culture is not always best understood or expressed in Western terms; conversely, Western culture and ideas can also seem alien and remote to the Japanese. Second, we should be aware, as Ellwood and Pilgrim observe, that Japanese religion is, above all, performed; it "is not fundamentally talk *about* the sacred nor even prayers *to* the sacred; above all it is heirophany—in Mircea Eliade's term— a showing of the sacred, both in itself and in the ultimately sacred structures of human life" (1985, 111). In every culture theatre and ritual are tied together; in Japan, the ritual is especially theatrical, and the theatre, particularly the traditional theatre, is highly stylized and ritualistic.

The modern theatre of Japan, however, does not have the stylization or ritual of the traditional religions. A product of Western influence, *shingeki* is the Japanese form of naturalism and realism as developed in Europe and the United States in the late nineteenth and early twentieth centuries. From its beginnings *shingeki* has been a Eurocentric drama, not influenced very much by traditional theatre or by traditional aesthetics except in reaction against them. Osanai Kaoru, Tsubouchi

Shoyo, and the other pioneers of the early modern theatre worked at creating what the name *shingeki* literally means: a "new theatre."

David Goodman notes in *Japanese Drama and Culture in the 1960s* that the two "main intellectual currents" that inform *shingeki* are Marxism and Christianity (1988, 17). The former's influence is evident in the plays of Kubo Sakae, the work of *Roen,* and the "socialist realist" plays that constituted left-wing *shingeki* from its origins through the postwar years. Less obvious perhaps is the influence of Christianity on modern Japanese drama, although, as Goodman notes, many modern Japanese dramatists (as well as actors and directors and audiences) have been Christians. Kishida Kunio, the father of the "Literary Theatre" (as opposed to "socialist theatre") movement was influenced by Jacques Copeau, who was actively interested in the combining of religion and theatre and who was fiercely Catholic (Rimer 1974, 59–60). "Kishida may have flirted with Catholicism himself," Goodman reports (1989, 20). Tanaka Chikao and Fukuda Tsuneari, Kishida's two main disciples, were both Catholics (Goodman 1988, 17; Ortolani 1971, 463). The Christian influence is present in plays by Kinoshita Junji, Satoh Makoto, Mushakoji Saneatsu, Akutagawa Ryunosuke, Arishima Takeo, Masamune Hakucho, Miyoshi Juro, Kato Michio, Sumie Tanaka, and Toshio Shimao, among others (Goodman 1988, n. 30; Phillips 1981, 126–27). And yet for the past century, Christians, on average, compose less than 1 percent of the Japanese population (Reid 1991, 7). The question is begged: why are there so many Christians involved in *shingeki?* What influence does this Western religion have on modern Japanese theatre, and why does it possess this influence?

Many Japanese Christians, such as the Reverend Yokoi Tokio and Uchimura Kanzo, founder of *Mukyokai* (the "Non-Church Movement"), advocate a "Japanese Christianity" free of Western influence. In this desire we see a tension that is manifest in all *shingeki* plays connected to Christianity: the artists and audiences explore "how to reconcile their Japanese identity with Western Culture" (Goodman and Miyazawa 1995, 40). I suggest that the key to understanding the influence of Christianity on the modern theatre lies in this very tension; the Christian *Shingeki* theatre artist explores the point of crisis between "being Japanese" and "being Christian." For some, there is no tension, no crisis. Uchimura declares that he is both: "an ellipse with two centers." Others, such as the novelist Endo Shusaku, explore the place of Christianity in Japan as a means to define both the self and the other, both the non-Japanese other and the non-Christian other. By belonging to both worlds, one might not truly belong to either. An examination of the issues surrounding the intellectual and cultural influences of Christianity on *shingeki* will illuminate the historical conditions that predispose *shingeki* to be linked to Christianity. Furthermore, discussion of Nakamura Kichizo's *Bokushi no ie,* Tanaka Chikao's *Maria no Kubi,* and Endo Shusaku's *Ogon no Kuni,* three plays by Christian playwrights, will reveal different ways in which the Christian and Japanese identities are synthesized within the plays.

Christianity, like Marxism, offers a nonindigenous intellectual framework from which the indigenous society may be explored critically. Like Marxism, Christianity claims to be acultural. Both have obvious Western roots, but they both claim universal status. They declare themselves nonelitist and, in fact, are ostensibly aimed at "the masses." During the 1930s both Marxism and Christianity provided "the strongest ideological opposition" to nationalism and militarism (Caldarola 1979, 164). Marxism, however, offers the specific goal of revolution as a solution to the problems of society. Left-wing *shingeki* plays offer a Marxist analysis of Japanese society and present revolution as the answer. Christian *shingeki,* however, does not have as easy a task defining both Japanese society and the place of Christians in it, nor as simple an answer to the social and cultural problems of Japan, particularly when less than 1 percent of the population is Christian (even that small percentage is split between Roman Catholic, Eastern Orthodox, and dozens of Protestant churches). Furthermore, many Japanese Christians are not members of any particular church but rather are "latent Christians" (Cooper 1983, 309), simply believing and worshiping individually or in family groups. Thus, there is little unity even among the few Christians in Japan.

However, the historical connection between Christianity and the Western culture that the Meiji Japanese sought to emulate provides a cultural force that more than compensates for the small number of actual Christians in Japan. Christianity was not imposed on Japan as part of a colonial culture but rather was embraced voluntarily, even enthusiastically, as the modern, Western, fashionable thing to do, thus avoiding the colonial stigma that it carries in other non-Western cultures. Christianity came to Japan in a variety of forms as part of the modernization effort by the Meiji government and intellectual elite. First, as noted above, the cultural models that Japan sought to build upon (art, literature, ethics, etc.) arose out of Europe's Christian heritage. Furthermore, the fascination with "things Western" during the Meiji era led to many students (intellectual youth and civil servants) converting to Christianity in an attempt to be more Western (Komiya 1956,

458). Western music, art, and drama were all introduced through Protestant hymns, books of moral lessons, religious paintings, and drama (Maus 1960, 715; Komiya 1956, 458). Father Nikolai, for whom the famous *Nikolai-do* is named, complained in one of his regular reports to the Moscow synod in 1887 that he was having difficulty finding converts to Russian Orthodox Christianity: "Catholic and Protestant countries have the power to captivate the Japanese, because the main stream of the civilization which Japanese are now endeavoring to absorb so rapidly and greedily has its origin in these countries. All kinds of theoretical and practical knowledge, all sorts of innovations and improvements, and numerous teachers come from these countries, and the . . . Japanese repeatedly renew their feelings of awe for these countries" (quoted in Naganawa 1995, 168). Christianity, for a brief while at least, ensured its popularity and fashionability because it was a gateway to the West and modernization.

Shingeki, as a product of Western influence, naturally has roots in Christianity. *Shingeki* critic and playwright Fukuda Tsuneari, for example, equated modernization with Christianity, as Ortolani notes: "For him [Fukuda] *shingeki* is the symbol of Japan's modernization as it brings into one arena the artistic and intellectual problems with which Japan has struggled for the past fifty years or more. . . . In Christianity, concretely in Catholicism, Fukuda recognizes the only spiritual, unifying force which can control modernization without denying it" (1971, 463, 482). Fukuda sees *shingeki* as embodying the modern and sees Christianity as the only intellectual current that controls and affirms modernization. For Fukuda, *shingeki* is a Christian theatre that, by following Western models, embodies Christianity onstage.

A second reason for Christianity's presence and influence is the predominance of Christian educational institutions, as well as the homogeneity of Christian communities and the *shingeki* audience base. From the Meiji era to the present day, Christians in Japan tend to be highly intellectual, educated, upper-middle-class urban elite with a cosmopolitan world view (Best 1966, 144; Goodman and Miyazawa 1995, 38; Reid 1991, n. 80; Scheiner 1970, 9). Such a description also applies to the average *shingeki* audience member. The higher level of education results from the fact that, from the Meiji era to the present day, education has been a special province of Christians in Japan. The early-nineteenth-century missionaries, arriving before the bans on Christianity were officially lifted, were teachers first and Christians second (Phillips 1981, 51). Yet, as both conscious and unconscious bearers of Western culture and beliefs, these teachers were the first to influence Japanese education with Christianity. Both those who make theatre and those who watch theatre were educated in Christian schools. In 1969, for example, 2,273 Christian schools (kindergarten through university) enrolled 655,722 students (not all of whom were Christians). The total Christian population of Japan at the time was 805,000; as James Phillips notes, when one considers the size of the Christian population "the size of the educational programs seems impressive indeed" (Phillips 1981, 50). Impressive and influential, one might add.

Thus, the importance of the Christian artistic heritage in the West, the intellectual heritage of *shingeki* as a theatre modeled on the Western drama, the influence of all things Western on the Japanese (particularly the young intellectuals who would create Japan's modern literature and drama), the use of Christianity as a nonindigenous intellectual framework from which one may critique Japanese culture, and the contributions of Christianity to Japanese education over the past century are all cultural forces that serve to connect *shingeki* to Christianity. These forces manifest themselves in different ways in three "test cases"—three plays written at different periods in the modern era by different Christian playwrights.

Christianity as a cultural phenomenon is implicit in much of the art and literature of the West. Chekhov, Strindberg, Shakespeare, and especially Ibsen served as models to the *shingeki* playwrights. In the case of Ibsen, Christianity is not the subject matter of the plays, but as Brian Johnston points out, "Hegelian Christianity" forms the intellectual focus and background of many of the plays of Ibsen's middle years (1992, 118–19). The characters of *The Wild Duck, Hedda Gabler, The Lady from the Sea,* and other such plays are concerned with issues of atonement, sin, guilt, and redemption. Several plays include pastors, ministers, and divinity students as main or supporting characters. Although no one would claim Ibsen was writing "Christian drama," his plays are nonetheless invested with a Christian intellectual background and the material culture as well as the religious occupations of nineteenth-century Christian Norway. These plays (with all of their attendant characters, ideas, and properties) form the models for *shingeki* playwrights.

An example of this Christian influence through the imitation of Ibsen can be found in Nakamura Kichizo's *Bokushi no ie,* translated as *A Vicarage,* but more properly translated as *A Vicar's House,* as Sato claims, for Nakamura was attempting to reflect Ibsen's *A Doll House* (1967, 441). Nakamura was one of Ibsen's strongest admirers in Meiji Japan, translating his work, using him as a model for his own experiments in dramaturgy, and writing the first definitive critical study of

Ibsen in Japanese. He was known as "Henrik Nakamura," so strongly was he identified with his subject (441).

Bokushi no ie presents the story of a Christian minister, Fujiwara Kakuichi, his second wife Kaneko, and her daughter Mariko, an atheist. In Ibsenesque style, the play unfolds to reveal the dark secrets hiding behind the bourgeois Meiji gentility of this family: Kaneko was a prostitute before she met Fujiwara, and Mariko is an illegitimate child whose father is unknown. Kaneko attempts suicide, unsuccessfully, at which point Mariko then reveals that she was responsible for the death of Shinichi, Fujiwara's only child from his first marriage, by convincing the frail child to climb to the top of the church steeple from which he slipped to his death (mimicking the fall of the child in *Little Eyolf*). She did this so that she would be the sole object of affection in her stepfather's eye, although Nakamura makes it clear that her love is more than merely filial. Fujiwara and Kaneko decide to open their home to the children of prostitutes as Mariko leaves for America. Fujiwara quits his post and renounces Christianity saying, "I no longer believe in God."

Nakamura's play is set in Japan and features a cast of Japanese characters. Yet the play itself is immersed in the Christian world—not only in its outward forms, set as it is in a vicarage and featuring a Christian minister as the main character, but also in its Hegelian philosophy and its discussions of sin and redemption. The play is set in a Japan that very much resembles nineteenth-century Norway. One wonders if Mrs. Alving or Judge Brack does not live next door to the Fujiwaras. By adapting the styles, themes, characters, and dialogue of Ibsen, the early *shingeki* brought Christianity to the fore as a theme, as a subject matter, and as a "stage dressing." Nakamura himself calls *Bokushi no ie* "the first 'war cry' of the *Shingeki* movement" (Sato 1967, 450), which implies that *shingeki*'s roots are in Ibsen's Christian soil.

Tanaka Chikao's *Maria no Kubi* (The Head of Mary) is in many ways the opposite of *Bokushi no ie*. Chikao's play follows no specific Western model and, in fact, through its poetic idiom even begins the move away from *shingeki* and toward *angura*. Rather than present a Japanese drama in Christian and Western terms, *Maria no Kubi* "expresses a Catholic theology using Buddhist terms and symbols" (Goodman 1994, 112). Subtitled *A Nagasaki Fantasia,* the play is set in Nagasaki after the dropping of the atomic bomb. It presents the story of a conspiracy of Catholics who plan to steal and rebuild the statue of Mary at Urakami Cathedral. The conspirators have all the pieces except the head of the Virgin, which is too heavy to move yet must be moved as the Cathedral is scheduled for demolition. They are led by Shika, a nurse and prostitute, and Shinobu, a housewife whose husband is bedridden (but not because of the bomb). Both Shika and Shinobu are Catholic, both are dedicated to Mary, and both have lives that seem to be disconnected from their Christianity. Shika is a prostitute. Shinobu yearns to kill a young thug named Jigoro because she feels he made her aware of her own fractured existence. All of the characters of the play lead "fractured existences" made symbolic in the broken statue of Mary. Shika cries out in a moment of desperation, "Mary! My Mary! / I want your head!" (142), as the rest of the statue has already been reassembled in Shika's home. Shika identifies herself with Mary's fractured state. Rimer claims that Shika and Mary both "yearn for wholeness" (1976, 288). Mary is called "the keloid Madonna" (279), whereas Shika herself has real keloid scars. Through faith and effort, all the characters struggle for a wholeness that in the end they seem to achieve, but the true outcome remains ambiguous. In the closing lines Shinobu finds the strength to lift the head of Mary after the statue speaks to the gathered group of Christians, but we do not see the statue restored, nor do we learn what happens to the Nagasaki Christians who conspire to save it. Instead, the audience has been given a message of faith: Mary has assured us that all will be well. God has not abandoned His flock but rather has used them to demonstrate His own power and love.

Tanaka, a Japanese Catholic himself, formulates a Christian response to what is both a Japanese and a Christian question: why did God allow Nagasaki, the most Christian city in Japan, to be bombed? This question had already been explored by Nagai Takashi in *Nagasaki no Kane* (The Bells of Nagasaki), although, as Goodman notes, Tanaka's response to the bombing is more subtle and complex than Nagai's (1994, 108). The bomb has fallen, but as with the persecutions of the past, martyrdom creates faith in those left behind. Rimer observes that "the faith, in the symbol of Mary's head, is to be taken in pieces and preserved again" (1976, 289). Experiencing the bomb has strengthened the faith of those who lived and made martyrs of those who died. In *Writing Ground Zero*, John Whittier Treat claims that the "irrepressible" theme in Nagasaki literature in general is the desire "to be a sacrifice, one consecrated not only for his fellow human beings, but for his abiding faith in the greater, unknowable designs of God" (1995, 313)—in short, martyrdom for the faith. *Maria no Kubi* is a prayer in praise of the new martyrs at Nagasaki. Ultimately, however, *Maria no Kubi* is a play that takes its Christian identity for granted and explores a Japanese issue from a Christian point of view. The play accepts both Japanese and Christians on their own terms and never sees the two as separate or mutually exclusive.

Other plays, however, dwell upon the tension between one's identity as a Christian and one's identity as a Japanese. The play that perhaps best engages this struggle between the Christian identity and the Japanese identity is Endo Shusaku's *Ogon no Kuni* (The Golden Country), which dramatizes the story of Christovao Ferriera, a subject Endo had already treated in novel form (*Chinmoku* [Silence] 1966). Whereas the novel's title indicates that the novel questions God's silence about the suffering of his people in Japan, the play deals specifically with two very different views of the place of Christianity in Japan.

The play begins at the Buddhist festival of O-Bon—the festival of the dead—in 1633 when the Tokugawa government has ordered all Christians to apostatize or face torture and execution. Inoue, Hirata, and other samurai are charged with ferreting out hidden Christians in Nagasaki. They suspect that some members of their own investigating group may be Christians themselves and they plan to trap them, but their ultimate goal is to catch Father Ferriera, a Jesuit hiding in the Nagasaki area and tending to the local Christians. He gives himself up, believing that his Japanese protector, Lord Tomonaga, a captured Christian undergoing torture in the pit, will be freed in exchange. Tomonaga, however, is already dead when Ferreira is brought to Inoue and Hirata. Much of the rest of the play is then occupied with Inoue's attempt to make Ferreira apostatize. At the heart of their struggle are two views of Japan: "The Mudswamp" and "The Golden Country." Ferreira sees Japan as "The Golden Country." To him Japan seems a place where Christianity would take root quickly and grow. The country seems beautiful and full of promise, although the persecutions give him another view of "The Golden Country." He tells Yuki, a young Christian girl, "Distant objects always seem beautiful. What is beyond reach always attracts. That is why one's memories are always beautiful" (55). Each martyr's death demonstrates the courage and faithfulness of Christians. In opposition to Ferreira is Inoue, who believes that Christianity will never grow in Japan. The samurai (and former Christian himself) sees Japan not as a "Golden Country," which he calls "just a dream," but as a "mudswamp": "Sometimes I get to dislike this country of ours. Or, more than dislike, to fear it. It's a mudswamp, much more frightening than what Christians call hell, this Japan. No matter what shoots one tries to transplant here from another country, they all wither and die, or else bear a flower and fruit that only resemble the real ones" (64).

Inoue sees Japan as incapable of accepting Christianity. He is astute enough to observe that the acculturation process changes the phenomenon or belief or idea that has crossed cultures. Christianity in Japan will take on a Japanese form, significantly different from its original form (indeed, one could say that Inoue was foreseeing the rise of *Mukyokai*). Even so, Inoue has his doubts: "Am I right? Or are the Christians right? Is Japan really a golden country in which the seed will grow, as Tomonaga says; or is it a swamp, as I think, a swamp in which the roots rot and die?" (70).

Through Inoue, Endo raises what may be the key issues in Christian *shingeki:* what is the place of Christianity in Japan? Can one be both Japanese and Christian? How does one identify oneself if one is both Japanese and Christian? These questions are just as valid to the non-Christian Japanese audience member, whose identity is also challenged in the course of the play: what does it mean to be Japanese? Ultimately, Endo may give us a few keys by which to examine more fully the role of Christianity in *shingeki,* beginning with this issue of identity. *Shingeki* gives both artist and audience a way to synthesize the two identities of the Japanese Christian. Second, as a Christian *and* as an artist, the *shingeki* playwright's responsibility is to "bear witness." This means not only to serve as a witness for his or her own personal beliefs but to "bear witness" about the problems, concerns, and issues of society. There is a moral drive, just as with the Marxist playwrights, to confront Japanese society with itself and ask questions that cannot be asked from within, only from without the society. The bearing of witness has been the past responsibility of Christian *shingeki* and will continue to be so.

Inoue, in *Ogon no kuni*, predicts a dire future for Christianity in Japan: that even though "the fathers" will return some day in the future, "what the Christians call the seed of God will not grow in this country" (70). He may be right. A recent article in the *New York Times* noted that Christianity is in decline in Japan, especially in the areas in Kyushu where hidden Christians have practiced their faith for years. For example, Ikitsuki Island, which had a 90 percent Christian population a century ago, is now only 10 percent Christian (Kristof 1997, A1). There are many reasons for this waning faith, a number of which are similar to those causing the decline of Christianity in the West: freedom of religion, the pressures of modern life, the influence of science and technology. *Shingeki*, too, like its Western counterpart, is in decline: audiences have decreased in number and fewer plays are being presented than twenty years ago. Still, in both cases, as "bearers of witness" and as intellectual owners of an outside view from which Japanese society and culture may be held up and critiqued, we can only hope (and perhaps pray) that their voices will continue to be lifted and heard. They will continue to dance at the shrines of Jesus and of Japan, an ellipse with two centers.

Works Cited

Best, Ernest E. 1966. *Christian Faith and Cultural Crisis: The Japanese Case.* Leiden: E. J. Brill.

Caldarola, Carlo. 1979. *Christianity: The Japanese Way.* Leiden: E. J. Brill.

Cieslik, Hubert. 1974. "The Case of Christovao Ferreira." *Monumenta Nipponica* 30, no. 1 (spring): 1–54.

Cooper, Michael. 1983. "Christianity." In *The Kodansha Encyclopedia of Japan.* Vol. 1. Tokyo: Kodansha.

Ellwood, Robert S., and Richard Pilgrim. 1985. *Japanese Religion.* Englewood Cliffs: Prentice-Hall.

Endo Shusaku. 1970. *The Golden Country.* Trans. Francis Mathy. Tokyo: Tuttle.

Goodman, David G., ed. 1988. *Japanese Drama and Culture in the 1960s.* Armonk: M. E. Sharpe.

———, ed. 1989. *Five Plays by Kishida Kunio.* Ithaca: Cornell University East Asia Papers.

———, ed. 1994. *After Apocalypse: Four Japanese Plays of Hiroshima and Nagasaki.* Ithaca: Cornell University East Asia Papers.

Goodman, David G., and Masanori Miyazawa. 1995. *Jews in the Japanese Mind.* New York: Free Press.

Johnston, Brian. 1992. *The Ibsen Cycle.* University Park: Pennsylvania State University Press.

Komiya Toyotaka, comp. and ed. 1956. *Japanese Music and Drama in the Meiji Era.* Trans. Edward G. Seidensticker and Donald Keene. Tokyo: Ôbunsha.

Kristof, Nicholas D. 1997. "Unpersecuted, an Old Faith Withers in Japan." *New York Times,* 3 April, sec. A, pp. 1, 9.

Maus, Cynthia Pearl. 1960. *The Church and the Fine Arts.* New York: Harper and Brothers.

Nagai Takashi. 1984. *The Bells of Nagasaki.* Trans. William Johnson. Tokyo: Kodansha.

Naganawa Mitsuo. 1995. "The Japanese Orthodox Church in the Meiji Era." In *A Hidden Fire: Russian and Japanese Cultural Encounters, 1868–1926,* ed. J. Thomas Rimer, 158–69. Stanford: Stanford University Press.

Nakamura Kichizo. 1910. *Bokushi no ie.* Tokyo: Shanjusha.

Ortolani, Benito. 1971. "Fukuda Tsuneari: Modernization and *Shingeki.*" In *Tradition and Modernization in Japanese Culture,* ed. Donald H. Shively, 463–99. Princeton: Princeton University Press.

Phillips, James M. 1981. *From the Rising of the Sun: Christians and Society in Contemporary Japan.* Mary Knoll: Orbis Books.

Reid, David. 1991. *New Wine: The Cultural Shaping of Japanese Christianity.* Berkeley: Asian Humanities Press.

Rimer, J. Thomas. 1974. *Toward a Modern Japanese Theatre*. Princeton: Princeton University Press.

——, ed. 1976. "Four Plays by Tanaka Chikao." *Monumenta Nipponica* 31, no. 3:275–98.

Sato, T. 1967. "Nakamura Kichizo's *A Vicarage* (1910) and Ibsen." *Modern Drama* 9 (February): 440–50.

Scheiner, Irwin. 1970. *Christian Converts and Social Protest in Meiji Japan*. Berkeley: University of California Press.

Treat, John Whittier. 1995. *Writing Ground Zero*. Chicago: University of Chicago Press.

Tsunoda Ryusaku, William Theodore deBary, and Donald Keene, eds. 1958. *Sources of Japanese Tradition*. Vol. 2. New York: Columbia University Press.

Contributors

James R. Brandon is the author of numerous books on Asian drama and theatre, including *The Cambridge Guide to Asian Theatre*. He directs notable *kabuki* plays at the University of Hawaii's Kennedy Theatre. He is the recipient of the prestigious J. D. Rockefeller III Award for contribution to the field of Asian Theatre Arts. He has also been awarded the Order of the Rising Sun by the Japanese government.

Carol Davis is an Assistant Professor in the Department of Theatre and Dance at Pomona College. She is also the founding director of the Nepal Health Project, which uses street theatre to address the health crisis in rural Nepal. Carol has toured throughout Nepal in a play she created with Nepali actors that has now been performed for over 30,000 villagers and students. Carol holds the Ph.D. degree from the University of California, Berkeley, where she wrote a dissertation on Shakespeare's cross-dressing heroines. She has acted at the Old Globe Theatre, San Diego Repertory Theatre, Berkeley Repertory Theatre, and the California Shakespeare Festival, among others. Carol has also directed plays at many theatres and schools including the California Young Playwrights Festival and the Washington Shakespeare Festival.

Samuel L. Leiter (Brooklyn College and the Graduate Center, CUNY) has been the editor of *Asian Theatre Journal* since 1992. He has published articles in many professional journals and chapters in eleven books. He is also author or editor of twelve books, the two most recent ones dealing with the Japanese stage: *The New Kabuki Encyclopedia: A*

Revised Adaptation of Kabuki Jiten and *Japanese Theatre in the World* (both 1997).

Paul Lifton is Associate Professor of Theatre Arts at North Dakota State University in Fargo. His activities encompass both scholarship and creative endeavor (primarily directing). His publications include *"Vast Encyclopedia": The Theatre of Thornton Wilder* (1995) and an essay in Martin Blank's anthology *Critical Essays on Thornton Wilder* (1996). He holds a Ph.D. in dramatic art from the University of California, Berkeley.

Claudia Orenstein received her Ph.D. from Stanford University in Directing and Criticism in Drama. She is currently Assistant Professor of Theatre at Barnard College in New York and has also taught at Pomona College in California. She has worked as an actress, director, and dramaturg. Her *Festive Revolutions: The Politics of Popular Theatre Forms* is being prepared for publication by the University Press of Mississippi in its Performance Studies series.

Leonard C. Pronko is Professor of Theatre at Pomona College. He is author of *Theatre East and West, Guide to Japanese Drama,* and a number of other books on Asian and European theatre. For the past thirty years, he has been directing *kabuki* in English and many Western plays in *kabuki* style, as well as Western plays in Western styles. In 1986 the government of Japan awarded him the Order of the Sacred Treasure.

Farley Richmond, Professor and Head of the Department of Drama, University of Georgia, is coauthor of *Indian Theatre: Traditions of Performance.* He is the author of numerous articles on classical, traditional, and contemporary Indian theatre and the forthcoming CD-ROM *Kutiyattam: Sanskrit Theatre of India,* University of Michigan Press.

Carol Fisher Sorgenfrei is a playwright, director, and translator/scholar of Japanese and cross-cultural theatre. She is a Professor of Theatre at UCLA, where she has served as head of the playwriting program and currently heads the Ph.D. program. She is the author of thirteen plays, many of them fusion plays, in which stylistic elements of classical Japanese theatre combine with classical Western themes and/or theatrical styles. Her research focuses upon Japanese theatre and especially the avant-garde playwright Shuji Terayama.

Min Tian holds a Ph.D. from China's Central Academy of Drama, where he has taught as a lecturer and an associate professor. He is now a Ph.D. candidate at the University of Illinois. He has published many scholarly articles on Shakespeare, modern drama, and intercultural theatre. His coauthored book, *Modern and Contemporary European Drama,* is forthcoming in China.

Andrew Tsubaki has his B.A. degree from Tokyo Gakugei, M.F.A. from Texas Christian University, and Ph.D. from the University of Illinois. He is on the faculty of the Department of Theatre and Film at the University of Kansas, where he is also Director of International Theatre Studies. He has published articles on Japanese and Indian theatre and has directed numerous theatrical productions merging Eastern and Western traditions such as *Rashomon, King Lear,* and *Hyppolytus.*

Kevin J. Wetmore, Jr., is completing his Ph.D. in theatre and performance studies at the University of Pittsburgh. In addition to being a professional actor and director, he studies and writes about contemporary Japanese and African theatre and about cross-cultural classical theatre.

Evan Winet is a graduate student in the Ph.D. program in drama at Stanford University and a freelance director and mask-maker. In 1996 he went to Bali with a group from the Dell'Arte School of Physical Theatre to explore crosscurrents between Balinese performance and Western physical theatre.